"Your Talk is Like the Wind"

"You, a penniless adventurer, say you can make me Emir of this city!" Alafdal Khan scowled menacingly at the lean stranger who stood before him. "I could have your head for such bold lies!"

The stranger folded his scarred, sinewy arms and spoke a single phrase—and Alafdal choked and lurched to his feet, reeling, his eyes searching the dark immobile face before him.

"Do you believe me now?"

"How could I not?" panted Alafdal. "You, who have put kings on their thrones. You, who have watered the desert with blood...And yet, you are mad to have come here!"

E. J. Fath.

Bed

39

SON OF
THE WHITE WOLF

ROBERT E. HOWARD

A BERKLEY BOOK
published by
BERKLEY PUBLISHING CORPORATION

SBN 425-03710-X

BERKLEY MEDALLION BOOKS are published by
Berkley Publishing Corporation
200 Madison Avenue
New York, N. Y. 10016

BERKLEY MEDALLION BOOK ® TM 757,375

Printed in the United States of America

Berkley Edition, APRIL, 1978

ACKNOWLEDGMENTS

Blood of the Gods, copyright 1935 by Street & Smith Publications, Inc. for *Top-Notch*, July 1935.

The Country of the Knife, copyright 1936 by Street & Smith Publications, Inc. for *Complete Stories*, August 1936.

Son of the White Wolf, copyright 1936 by Metropolitan Magazines, Inc. for *Thrilling Adventures*, December 1936.

CONTENTS

Blood of the Gods

CHAPTER 1.

A Shot Through the Window

IT WAS THE wolfish snarl on Hawkston's thin lips, the red glare in his eyes, which first roused terrified suspicion in the Arab's mind, there in the deserted hut on the outskirts of the little town of Azem. Suspicion became certainty as he stared at the three dark, lowering faces of the other white men, bent toward him, and all beastly with the same cruel greed that twisted their leader's features.

The brandy glass slipped from the Arab's hand and his swarthy skin went ashy.

"*Lah*!" he cried desperately. "No! You lied to me! You are not friends—you brought me here to murder me—"

He made a convulsive effort to rise, but Hawkston grasped the bosom of his *gumbaz* in an iron grip and forced him down into the camp chair again. The Arab cringed away from the dark, hawk-like visage bending close to his own.

"You won't be hurt, Dirdar," rasped the Englishman. "Not if you tell us what we want to know. You heard my question. Where is Al Wazir?"

The beady eyes of the Arab glared wildly up at his

captor for an instant, then Dirdar moved with all the strength and speed of his wiry body. Bracing his feet against the floor, he heaved backward suddenly, toppling the chair over and throwing himself along with it. With a rending of worn cloth the bosom of the *gumbaz* came away in Hawkston's hand, and Dirdar, regaining his feet like a bouncing rubber ball, dived straight at the open door, ducking beneath the pawing arm of the big Dutchman, Van Brock. But he tripped over Ortelli's extended leg and fell sprawling, rolling on his back to slash up at the Italian with the curved knife he had snatched from his girdle. Ortelli jumped back, yowling, blood spurting from his leg, but as Dirdar once more bounced to his feet, the Russian, Krakovitch, struck him heavily from behind with a pistol barrel.

As the Arab sagged to the floor, stunned, Hawkston kicked the knife out of his hand. The Englishman stooped, grabbed him by the collar of his *abba*, and grunted: "Help me lift him, Van Brock."

The burly Dutchman complied, and the half-senseless Arab was slammed down in the chair from which he had just escaped. They did not tie him, but Krakovitch stood behind him, one set of steely fingers digging into his shoulder, the other poising the long gun-barrel.

Hawkston poured out a glass of brandy and thrust it to his lips. Dirdar gulped mechanically, and the glassiness faded out of his eyes.

"He's coming around," grunted Hawkston. "You hit him hard, Krakovitch. Shut up, Ortelli! Tie a rag about your bally leg and quit grousing about it! Well, Dirdar, are you ready to talk?"

The Arab looked about like a trapped animal, his lean chest heaving under the torn *gumbaz*. He saw no mercy in the flinty faces about him.

"Let's burn his cursed feet," snarled Ortelli, busy with an improvised bandage. "Let me put the hot irons to the swine—"

Dirdar shuddered and his gaze sought the face of the Englishman, with burning intensity. He knew that

Hawkston was leader of these lawless men by virtue of sharp wits and a sledge-like fist.

The Arab licked his lips.

"As Allah is my witness, I do not know where Al Wazir is!"

"You lie!" snapped the Englishman. "We know that you were one of the party that took him into the desert—and he never came back. We know you know where he was left. Now, are you going to tell?"

"El Borak will kill me!" muttered Dirdar.

"Who's El Borak?" rumbled Van Brock.

"American," snapped Hawkston. "Adventurer. Real name's Gordon. He led the caravan that took Al Wazir into the desert. Dirdar, you needn't fear El Borak. We'll protect you from him."

A new gleam entered the Arab's shifty eyes; avarice mingled with the fear already there. Those beady eyes grew cunning and cruel.

"There is only one reason why you wish to find Al Wazir," he said. "You hope to learn the secret of a treasure richer than the secret hoard of Shahrazar the Forbidden! Well, suppose I tell you? Suppose I even guide you to the spot where Al Wazir is to be found—will you protect me from El Borak—will you give me a share of the Blood of the Gods?"

Hawkston frowned, and Ortelli ripped out an oath.

"Promise the dog nothing! Burn the soles off his feet! Here! I'll heat the irons!"

"Let that alone!" said Hawkston with an oath. "One of you better go to the door and watch. I saw that old devil Salim sneaking around through the alleys just before sundown."

No one obeyed. They did not trust their leader. He did not repeat the command. He turned to Dirdar, in whose eyes greed was much stronger now than fear.

"How do I know you'd guide us right? Every man in that caravan swore an oath he'd never betray Al Wazir's hiding place."

"Oaths were made to be broken," answered Dirdar

cynically. "For a share in the Blood of the Gods I would foreswear Muhammad. But even when you have found Al Wazir, you may not be able to learn the secret of the treasure."

"We have ways of making men talk," Hawkston assured him grimly. "Will you put our skill to the test, or will you guide us to Al Wazir? We will give you a share of the treasure." Hawkston had no intention of keeping his word as he spoke.

"*Mashallah!*" said the Arab. "He dwells alone in an all but inaccessible place. When I name it, you, at least, Hawkston *effendi*, will know how to reach it. But I can guide you by a shorter way, which will save two days. And a day saved on the desert is often the difference between life and death.

"Al Wazir dwells in the Caves of El Khour—arrrgh!" His voice broke in a scream, and he threw up his hands, a sudden image of frantic terror, eyes glaring, teeth bared. Simultaneously the deafening report of a shot filled the hut, and Dirdar toppled from his chair, clutching at his breast. Hawkston whirled, caught a glimpse through the window of a smoking black pistol barrel and a grim bearded face. He fired at that face even as, with his left hand, he swept the candle from the table and plunged the hut into darkness.

His companions were cursing, yelling, falling over each other, but Hawkston acted with unerring decision. He plunged to the door of the hut, knocking aside somebody who stumbled into his path, and threw the door open. He saw a figure running across the road, into the shadows on the side. He threw up his revolver, fired, and saw the figure sway and fall headlong, to be swallowed up by the darkness under the trees. He crouched for an instant in the doorway, gun lifted, left arm barring the blundering rush of the other men.

"Keep back, curse you! That was old Salim. There may be more, under the trees across the road."

But no menacing figure appeared, no sound mingled with the rustling of the palm-leaves in the wind, except a noise that might have been a man flopping in his death-throes—or dragging himself painfully away on hands and knees. This noise quickly ceased and Hawkston stepped cautiously out into the starlight. No shot greeted his appearance, and instantly he became a dynamo of energy. He leaped back into the hut, snarling: "Van Brock, take Ortelli and look for Salim. I know I hit him. You'll probably find him lying dead over there under the trees. If he's still breathing, finish him! He was Al Wazir's steward. We don't want him taking tales to Gordon."

Followed by Krakovitch, the Englishman groped his way into the darkened hut, struck a light and held it over the prostrate figure on the floor; it etched a grey face, staring glassy eyes, and a naked breast in which showed a round blue hole from which the blood had already ceased to ooze.

"Shot through the heart!" swore Hawkston, clenching his fist. "Old Salim must have seen him with us, and trailed him, guessing what we were after. The old devil shot him to keep him from guiding us to Al Wazir—but no matter. I don't need any guide to get me to the Caves of El Khour—well?" As the Dutchman and the Italian entered.

Van Brock spoke: "We didn't find the old dog. Smears of blood all over the grass, though. He must have been hard hit."

"Let him go," snarled Hawkston. "He's crawled away to die somewhere. It's a mile to the nearest occupied house. He won't live to get that far. Come on! The camels and the men are ready. They're behind that palm grove south of this hut. Everything's ready for the jump, just as I planned it. Let's go!"

Soon thereafter there sounded the soft pad of camel's hoofs and the jingle of accoutrements, as a line of mounted figures, ghostly in the night, moved westward into the desert. Behind them the flat roofs of el-Azem slept in the starlight, shadowed by the palm-leaves which stirred in the breeze that blew from the Persian Gulf.

CHAPTER 2.

The Abodes of Emptiness

GORDON'S THUMB WAS hooked easily in his belt, keeping his hand near the butt of his heavy pistol, as he rode leisurely through the starlight, and his gaze swept the palms which lined each side of the road, their broad fronds rattling in the faint breeze. He did not expect an ambush or the appearance of an enemy. He had no blood-feud with any man in el-Azem. And yonder, a hundred yards ahead of him, stood the flat-roofed, wall-encircled house of his friend, Achmet ibn Mitkhal, where the American was living as an honored guest. But the habits of a life-time are tenacious. For years El Borak had carried his life in his hands, and if there were hundreds of men in Arabia proud to call him friend, there were hundreds of others who would have given the teeth out of their heads for a clean sight of him, etched against the stars, over the barrel of a rifle.

Gordon reached the gate, and was about to call to the gate-keeper, when it swung open, and the portly figure of his host emerged.

"Allah be with thee, El Borak! I was beginning to fear

some enemy had laid an ambush for you. Is it wise to ride alone, by night, when within a three days' ride dwell men who bear blood-feud with you?"

Gordon swung down, and handed his reins to a groom who had followed his master out of the compound. The American was not a large man, but he was square-shouldered and deep-chested, with corded sinews and steely nerves which had been tempered and honed by the tooth-and-nail struggle for survival in the wild outlands of the world. His black eyes gleamed in the starlight like those of some untamed son of the wilderness.

"I think my enemies have decided to let me die of old age or inertia," he replied. "There has not been—"

"What's that?" Achmet ibn Mitkhal had his own enemies. In an instant the curious dragging, choking sounds he had heard beyond the nearest angle of the wall had transformed him into a tense image of suspicion and menace.

Gordon had heard the sounds as quickly as his Arab host, and he turned with the smooth speed of a cat, the big pistol appearing in his right hand as if by magic. He took a single quick stride toward the angle of the wall—then around that angle came a strange figure, with torn, trailing garments. A man, crawling slowly and painfully along on his hands and knees. As he crawled he gasped and panted with a grisly whistling and gagging in his breathing. As they stared at him, he slumped down almost at their feet, turning a blood-streaked visage to the starlight.

"Salim!" ejaculated Gordon softly, and with one stride he was at the angle, staring around it, pistol poised. No living thing met his eye; only an expanse of bare ground, barred by the shadows of the palms. He turned back to the prostrate man, over whom Achmet was already bending.

"*Effendi!*" panted the old man. "El Borak!" Gordon dropped to his knee beside him, and Salim's bony fingers clenched desperately on his arm.

"A *hakim*, quick, Achmet!" snapped Gordon.

"Nay," gasped Salim. "I am dying—"

"Who shot you, Salim?" asked Gordon, for he had already ascertained the nature of the wound which dyed the old man's tattered *abba* with crimson.

"Hawkston—the Englishman." The words came with an effort. "I saw him—the three rogues who follow him—beguiling that fool Dirdar to the deserted hut near Mekmet's Pool. I followed for I knew—they meant no good. Dirdar was a dog. He drank liquor—like an Infidel. El Borak! He betrayed Al Wazir! In spite of his oath. I shot him—through the window—but not in time. He will never guide them—but he told Hawkston—of the Caves of El Khour. I saw their caravan—camels—seven Arab servants. El Borak! They have departed—for the Caves—the Caves of El Khour!"

"Don't worry about them, Salim," replied Gordon, responding to the urgent appeal in the glazing eyes. "They'll never lay hand on Al Wazir. I promise you."

"*Al Hamud Lillah*—" whispered the old Arab, and with a spasm that brought frothy blood to his bearded lips, his grim old face set in iron lines, and he was dead before Gordon could ease his head to the ground.

The American stood up and looked down at the silent figure. Achmet came close to him and tugged his sleeve.

"Al Wazir!" murmured Achmet. "*Wallah*! I thought men had forgotten all about that man. It is more than a year now since he disappeared."

"White men don't forget—not when there's loot in the offing," answered Gordon sardonically. "All up and down the coast men are still looking for the Blood of the Gods—those marvelous matched rubies which were Al Wazir's especial pride, and which disappeared when he forsook the world and went into the desert to live as a hermit, seeking the Way to Truth through meditation and self-denial."

Achmet shivered and glanced westward where, beyond the belt of palms, the shadowy desert stretched vast and mysterious to mingle its immensity with the dimness of the starlit night.

"A hard way to seek Truth," said Achmet, who was a

lover of the soft things and the rich things of life.

"Al Wazir was a strange man," answered Gordon. "But his servants loved him. Old Salim there, for instance. Good God, Mekmet's Pool is more than a mile from here. Salim crawled—crawled all that way, shot through and through. He knew Hawkston would torture Al Wazir—maybe kill him. Achmet, have my racing camel saddled—"

"I'll go with you!" exclaimed Achmet. "How many men will we need? You heard Salim—Hawkston will have at least eleven men with him—"

"We couldn't catch him now," answered Gordon. "He's got too much of a start on us. His camels are *hejin*—racing camels—too. I'm going to the Caves of El Khour, alone."

"But—"

"They'll go by the caravan road that leads to Riyadh; I'm going by the Well of Amir Khan."

Achmet blenched.

"Amir Khan lies within the country of Shalan ibn Mansour, who hates you as an *iman* hates *Shaitan* the Damned!"

"Perhaps none of his tribe will be at the Well," answered Gordon. "I'm the only *Feringhi* who knows of that route. If Dirdar told Hawkston about it, the Englishman couldn't find it, without a guide. I can get to the Caves a full day ahead of Hawkston. I'm going alone, because we couldn't take enough men to whip the Ruweila if they're on the war-path. One man has a better chance of slipping through than a score. I'm not going to fight Hawkston—not now. I'm going to warn Al Wazir. We'll hide until Hawkston gives it up and comes back to el-Azem. Then, when he's gone, I'll return by the caravan road."

Achmet shouted an order to the men who were gathering just within the gate, and they scampered to do his bidding.

"You will go disguised, at least?" he urged.

"No. It wouldn't do any good. Until I get into Ruweila

country I won't be in any danger, and after that a disguise would be useless. The Ruweila kill and plunder every stranger they catch, whether Christian or Muhammadan."

He strode into the compound to oversee the saddling of the white racing camel.

"I'm riding light as possible," he said. "Speed means everything. The camel won't need any water until we reach the Well. After that it's not a long jump to the Caves. Load on just enough food and water to last me to the Well, with economy."

His economy was that of a true son of the desert. Neither water-skin nor food-bag was over-heavy when the two were slung on the high rear pommel. With a brief word of farewell, Gordon swung into the saddle, and at the tap of his bamboo stick, the beast lurched to its feet. "Yahh!" Another tap and it swung into motion. Men pulled wide the compound gate and stood aside, their eyes gleaming in the torchlight.

"*Bismillah el rahman el rahhim*!" quoth Achmet resignedly, lifting his hands in a gesture of benediction, as the camel and its rider faded into the night.

"He rides to death," muttered a bearded Arab.

"Were it another man I should agree," said Achmet. "But it is El Borak who rides. Yet Shalan ibn Mansour would give many horses for his head."

The sun was swinging low over the desert, a tawny stretch of rocky soil and sand as far as Gordon could see in every direction. The solitary rider was the only visible sign of life, but Gordon's vigilance was keen. Days and nights of hard riding lay behind him; he was coming into the Ruweila country, now, and every step he took increased his danger by that much. The Ruweila, whom he believed to be kin to the powerful Roualla of El Hamad, were true sons of Ishmael—hawks of the desert, whose hands were against every man not of their clan. To avoid their country the regular caravan road to the west swung wide to the south. This was an easy route, with wells a day's march apart, and it passed within a day's ride of the Caves of El Khour, the catacombs which pit a low range of hills rising sheer out of the wastelands.

Few white men know of their existence, but evidently Hawkston knew of the ancient trail that turned northward from the Well of Khosru, on the caravan road. Hawkston was perforce approaching El Khour circuitously. Gordon was heading straight westward, across waterless wastes, cut by a trace so faint only an Arab or El Borak could have followed it. On that route there was but one watering place between the fring of oases along the coast and the Caves—the half-mythical Well of Amir Khan, the existence of which was a secret jealously guarded by the Bedouins.

There was no fixed habitation at the oasis, which was but a clump of palms, watered by a small spring, but frequently bands of Ruweila camped there. That was a chance he must take. He hoped they were driving their camel herds somewhere far to the north, in the heart of their country; but like true hawks, they ranged far afield, striking at the caravans and the outlying villages.

The trail he was following was so slight that few would have recognized it as such. It stretched dimly away before him over a level expanse of stone-littered ground, broken on one hand by sand dunes, on the other by a succession of low ridges. He glanced at the sun, and tapped the water-bag that swung from the saddle. There was little left, though he had practiced the grim economy of a Bedouin or a wolf. But within a few hours he would be at the Well of Amir Khan, where he would replenish his supply—though his nerves tightened at the thought of what might be waiting there for him.

Even as the thought passed through his mind, the sun struck a glint from something on the nearer of the sand dunes. The quick duck of his head was instinctive, and simultaneously there rang out the crack of a rifle and he heard the thud of the bullet into flesh. The camel leaped convulsively and came down in a headlong sprawl, shot through the heart. Gordon leaped free as it fell, rifle in hand, and in an instant was crouching behind the carcass, watching the crest of the dune over the barrel of his rifle. A strident yell greeted the fall of the camel, and another shot set the echoes barking. The bullet ploughed into the ground beside Gordon's stiffening breastwork, and the American replied. Dust spurted into the air so near the muzzle that gleamed on the crest that it evoked a volley of lurid oaths in a choked voice.

The black glittering ring was withdrawn, and presently there rose the rapid drum of hoofs. Gordon saw a white *kafieh* bobbing among the dunes, and understood the Bedouin's plan. He believed there was only one man. That man intended to circle Gordon's position, cross the trail a few hundred yards west of him, and get on the rising ground behind the American, where his vantage-point would allow him to shoot over the bulk of the camel—for of course he knew Gordon would keep the dead beast between them. But Gordon shifted himself only enough to command the trail ahead of him, the open space the Arab must cross after leaving the dunes before he reached the protection of the ridges. Gordon rested his rifle across the stiff forelegs of the camel.

A quarter of a mile up the trail there was a sandstone rock jutting up in the skyline. Anyone crossing the trail between it and himself would be limned against it momentarily. He set his sights and drew a bead against that rock. He was betting that the Bedouin was alone, and that he would not withdraw to any great distance before making the dash across the trail.

Even as he meditated a white-clad figure burst from among the ridges and raced across the trail, bending low in the saddle and flogging his mount. It was a long shot, but Gordon's nerves did not quiver. At the exact instant that the white-clad figure was limned against the distant rock, the American pulled the trigger. For a fleeting moment he thought he had missed; then the rider straightened convulsively, threw up two wide-sleeved arms and reeled back drunkenly. The frightened horse reared high, throwing the man heavily. In an instant the landscape showed two separate shapes where there had been one—a bundle of white sprawling on the ground, and a horse racing off southward.

Gordon lay motionless for a few minutes, too wary to expose himself. He knew the man was dead; the fall alone would have killed him. But there was a slight chance that other riders might be lurking among the sand dunes, after all.

The sun beat down savagely; vultures appeared from nowhere—black dots in the sky, swinging in great circles, lower and lower. There was no hint of movement among the ridges or the dunes.

Gordon rose and glanced down at the dead camel. His jaws set a trifle more grimly; that was all. But he realized what the killing of his steed meant. He looked westward, where the heat waves shimmered. It would be a long walk, a long, dry walk, before it ended.

Stooping, he unslung water-skin and food-bag and threw them over his shoulders. Rifle in hand he went up the trail with a steady, swinging stride that would eat up the miles and carry him for hour after hour without faltering.

When he came to the shape sprawling in the path, he set the butt of his rifle on the ground and stood looking briefly, one hand steadying the bags on his shoulders. The man he had killed was a Ruweila, right enough: one of the tall, sinewy, hawk-faced and wolf-hearted plunderers of the southern desert. Gordon's bullet had caught him just below the arm-pit. That the man had been alone, and on a horse instead of a camel, meant that there was a larger party of his tribesmen somewhere in the vicinity. Gordon shrugged his shoulders, shifted the rifle to the crook of his arm, and moved on up the trail. The score between himself and the men of Shalan ibn Mansour was red enough, already. It might well be settled once and for all at the Well of Amir Khan.

As he swung along the trail he kept thinking of the man he was going to warn: Al Wazir, the Arabs called him, because of his former capacity with the Sultan of Oman. A Russian nobleman, in reality, wandering over the world

in search of some mystical goal Gordon had never
understood, just as an unquenchable thirst for adventure
drove El Borak around the planet in constant wanderings.
But the dreamy soul of the Slav coveted something more
than material things. Al Wazir had been many things.
Wealth, power, position; all had slipped through his
unsatisfied fingers. He had delved deep in strange
religions and philosophies, seeking the answer to the
riddle of Existence, as Gordon sought the stimulation of
hazard. The mysticisms of the Sufia had attracted him,
and finally the ascetic mysteries of the Hindus.

A year before Al Wazir had been governor of Oman,
next to the Sultan the wealthiest and most powerful man
on the Pearl Coast. Without warning he had given up his
position and disappeared. Only a chosen few knew that he
had distributed his vast wealth among the poor,
renounced all ambition and power, and gone like an
ancient prophet to dwell in the desert, where, in the
solitary meditation and self-denial of a true ascetic, he
hoped to read at last the eternal riddle of Life—as the
ancient prophets read it. Gordon had accompanied him
on that last journey, with the handful of faithful servants
who knew their master's intentions—old Salim among
them, for between the dreamy philosopher and the hard-
bitten man of action there existed a powerful tie of
friendship.

But for the traitor and fool, Dirdar, Al Wazir's secret
had been well kept. Gordon knew that ever since Al
Wazir's disappearance, adventurers of every breed had
been searching for him, hoping to secure possession of the
treasure that the Russian had possessed in the days of his
power—the wonderful collection of perfectly matched
rubies, known as the Blood of the Gods, which had blazed
a lurid path through Oriental history for five hundred
years. These jewels had not been distributed among the
poor with the rest of Al Wazir's wealth. Gordon himself
did not know what the man had done with them. Nor did
the American care. Greed was not one of his faults. And
Al Wazir was his friend.

The blazing sun rocked slowly down the sky, its flame turned to molten copper; it touched the desert rim, and etched against it, a crawling black tiny figure, Gordon moved grimly on, striding inexorably into the somber immensities of the Ruba al Khali—the Empty Abodes.

CHAPTER 3.

The Fight at the Well of Amir Khan

ETCHED AGAINST A white streak of dawn, motionless as figures on a tapestry, Gordon saw the clump of palms that marked the Well of Amir Khan grow up out of the fading night.

A few moments later he swore, softly. Luck, the fickle jade, was not with him this time. A faint ribbon of blue smoke curled up against the whitening sky. There were men at the Well of Amir Khan.

Gordon licked his dry lips. The water-bag that slapped against his back at each stride was flat, empty. The distance he would have covered in a matter of hours, skimming over the desert on the back of his tireless camel, he had trudged on foot, the whole night long, even though he had held a gait that few even of the desert's sons could have maintained unbroken. Even for him, in the coolness of the night, it had been a hard trek, though his iron muscles resisted fatigue like a wolf's.

Far to the east a low blue line lay on the horizon. It was the range of hills that held the Caves of El Khour. He was still ahead of Hawkston, forging on somewhere far to the south. But the Englishman would be gaining on him at every stride. Gordon could swing wide to avoid the men at the Well, and trudge on. Trudge on, afoot, and with empty water-bag? It would be suicide. He could never reach the Caves on foot and without water. Already he was bitten by the devils of thirst.

A red flame grew up in his eyes, and his dark face set in wolfish lines. Water was life in the desert; life for him and for Al Wazir. There was water at the Well, and camels. There were men, his enemies, in possession of both. If they lived, he must die. It was the law of the wolf-pack, and of the desert. He slipped the limp bags from his shoulders, cocked his rifle and went forward to kill or be killed—not for wealth, nor the love of a woman, nor an ideal, nor a dream, but for as much water as could be carried in a sheep-skin bag.

A *wadi* or gully broke the plain ahead of him, meandering to a point within a few hundred feet of the Well. Gordon crept toward it, taking advantage of every bit of cover. He had almost reached it, at a point a hundred yards from the Well, when a man in white *kafieh* and ragged *abba* materialized from among the palms. Discovery in the growing light was instant. The Arab yelled and fired. The bullet knocked up dust a foot from Gordon's knee, as he crouched on the edge of the gully, and he fired back. The Arab cried out, dropped his rifle and staggered drunkenly back among the palms.

The next instant Gordon had sprung down into the gully and was moving swiftly and carefully along it, toward the point where it bent nearest the Well. He glimpsed white-clad figures flitting briefly among the trees, and then rifles began to crack viciously. Bullets sang over the gully as the men fired from behind their saddles and bales of goods, piled like a rampart among the stems of the palms. They lay in the eastern fringe of the clump; the camels, Gordon knew, were on the other side of the trees. From the volume of the firing it could not be a large party.

A rock on the edge of the gully provided cover. Gordon

thrust his rifle barrel under a jutting corner of it and watched for movement among the palms. Fire spurted and a bullet whined off the rock—zingggg! Dwindling in the distance like the dry whir of a rattler. Gordon fired at the puff of smoke, and a defiant yell answered him.

His eyes were slits of black flame. A fight like this could last for days. And he could not endure a siege. He had no water; he had no time. A long march to the south the caravan of Hawkston was swinging relentlessly westward, each step carrying them nearer the Caves of El Khour and the unsuspecting man who dreamed his dreams there. A few hundred feet away from Gordon there was water, and camels that would carry him swiftly to his destination; but lead-fanged wolves of the desert lay between.

Lead came at his retreat thick and fast, and vehement voices rained maledictions on him. They let him know they knew he was alone, and on foot, and probably half-mad with thirst. They howled jeers and threats. But they did not expose themselves. They were confident but wary, with the caution taught by the desert deep ingrained in them. They held the winning hand and they intended to keep it so.

An hour of this, and the sun climbing over the eastern rim, and the heat beginning—the molten, blinding heat of the southern desert. It was fierce already; later it would be a scorching hell in that unshielded gully. Gordon licked his blackened lips and staked his life and the life of Al Wazir on one desperate cast of Fate's blind dice.

Recognizing and accepting the terrible odds against success, he raised himself high enough to expose head and one shoulder above the gully rim, firing as he did so. Three rifles cracked together and lead hummed about his ears; the bullet of one raked a white-hot line across his upper arm. Instantly Gordon cried out, the loud, agonized cry of a man hard hit, and threw his arms above the rim of the gully in the convulsive gesture of a man suddenly death-stricken. One hand held the rifle and the motion threw it out of the gully, to fall ten feet away, in plain sight of the Arabs.

An instant's silence, in which Gordon crouched below the rim, then blood-thirsty yells echoed his cry. He dared not raise himself high enough to look, but he heard the slap-slap-slap of sandalled feet, winged by hate and blood-lust. They had fallen for his ruse. Why not? A crafty man might feign a wound and fall, but who would deliberately cast away his rifle? The thought of a *Feringhi*, lying helpless and badly wounded in the bottom of the gully, with a defenseless throat ready for the knife, was too much for the blood-lust of the Bedouins. Gordon held himself in iron control, until the swift feet were only a matter of yards away—then he came erect like a steel spring released, the big automatic in his hand.

As he leaped up he caught one split-second glimpse of three Arabs, halting dead in their tracks, wild-eyed at the unexpected apparition—even as he straightened his gun was roaring. One man spun on his heel and fell in a crumpled heap, shot through the head. Another fired once, with a rifle, from the hip, without aim. An instant later he was down, with a slug through his groin and another ripping through his breast as he fell. And then Fate took a hand again—Fate in the form of a grain of sand in the mechanism of Gordon's automatic. The gun jammed just as he threw it down on the remaining Arab.

This man had no gun; only a long knife. With a howl he wheeled and legged it back for the grove, his rags whipping on the wind of his haste. And Gordon was after him like a starving wolf. His strategy might go for nothing if the man got back among the trees, where he might have left a rifle.

The Bedouin ran like an antelope, but Gordon was so close behind him when they reached the trees, the Arab had no time to snatch up the rifle leaning against the improvised rampart. He wheeled at bay, yowling like a mad dog, and slashing with the long knife. The point tore Gordon's shirt as the American dodged, and brought down the heavy pistol on the Arab's head. The thick *kafieh* saved the man's skull from being crushed, but his knees buckled and he went down, throwing his arms about Gordon's waist and dragging down the white man as he fell. Somewhere on the other side of the grove the wounded man was calling down curses on El Borak.

The two men rolled on the ground, ripping and smiting like wild animals. Gordon struck once again with his gun barrel, a glancing blow that laid open the Arab's face from eye to jaw, and then dropped the jammed pistol and caught at the arm that wielded the knife. He got a grip with his left hand on the wrist and the guard of the knife itself, and with his other hand began to fight for a throat-hold. The Arab's ghastly, blood-smeared countenance writhed in a tortured grin of muscular strain. He knew the terrible strength that lurked in El Borak's iron fingers, knew that if they closed on his throat they would not let go until his jugular was torn out.

He threw his body frantically from side to side, wrenching and tearing. The violence of his efforts sent both men rolling over and over, to crash against palm stems and carom against saddles and bales. Once Gordon's head was driven hard against a tree, but the blow did not weaken him, nor did the vicious drive the Arab got in with a knee to his groin. The Bedouin grew frantic, maddened by the fingers that sought his throat, the dark face, inexorable as iron, that glared into his own. Somewhere on the other side of the grove a pistol was barking, but Gordon did not feel the tear of lead, nor hear the whistle of bullets.

With a shriek like a wounded panther's, the Arab whirled over again, a knot of straining muscles, and his hand, thrown out to balance himself, fell on the barrel of the pistol Gordon had dropped. Quick as a flash he lifted it, just as Gordon found the hold he had been seeking, and crashed the butt down on the American's head with every ounce of strength in his lean sinews, backed by the fear of death. A tremor ran through the American's iron frame, and his head fell forward. And in that instant the Ruweila tore free like a wolf breaking from a trap, leaving his long knife in Gordon's hand.

Even before Gordon's brain cleared, his war-trained muscles were responding instinctively. As the Ruweila sprang up, he shook his head and rose more slowly, the long knife in his hand. The Arab hurled the pistol at him, and caught up the rifle which leaned against the barrier. He gripped it by the barrel with both hands and wheeled, whirling the stock above his head; but before the blow could fall Gordon struck with all the blinding speed that had earned him his name among the tribes. In under the descending butt he lunged and his knife, driven with all his strength and the momentum of his charge, plunged into the Arab's breast and drove him back against a tree into which the blade sank a hand's breadth deep. The Bedouin cried out, a thick, choking cry that death cut short. An instant he sagged against the haft, dead on his feet and nailed upright to the palm tree. Then his knees buckled and his weight tore the knife from the wood and he pitched into the sand.

Gordon wheeled, shaking the sweat from his eyes, glaring about for the fourth man—the wounded man. The furious fight had taken only a matter of moments. The pistol was still cracking dryly on the other side of the trees, and an animal scream of pain mingled with the reports.

With a curse Gordon caught up the Arab's rifle and burst through the grove. The wounded man lay under the shade of the trees, propped on an elbow, and aiming his pistol, not at El Borak but at the one camel that still lived. The other three lay stretched in their blood. Gordon sprang at the man, swinging the rifle stock. He was a split-second too late. The shot cracked and the camel moaned and crumpled even as the butt fell on the lifted arm, snapping the bone like a twig. The smoking pistol fell into the sand and the Arab sank back, laughing like a ghoul.

"Now see if you can escape from the Well of Amir Khan, El Borak!" he gasped. "The riders of Shalan ibn Mansour are out! Tonight or tomorrow they will return to the Well! Will you await them here, or flee on foot to die in the desert, or be tracked down like a wolf? *Ya kalb!* Forgotten of God! They will hang thy skin on a palm-tree! *Laan' abuk*—!"

Lifting himself with an effort that spattered his beard

with bloody foam, he spat toward Gordon, laughed croakingly and fell back, dead before his head hit the ground.

Gordon stood like a statue, staring down at the dying camels. The dead man's vengeance was grimly characteristic of his race. Gordon lifted his head and looked long at the low blue range on the western horizon. Cheeringly the dying Arab had foretold the grim choice left him. He could wait at the Well until Shalan ibn Mansour's wild riders returned and wiped him out by force of numbers, or he could plunge into the desert again on foot. And whether he awaited certain doom at the Well, or sought the uncertain doom of the desert, inexorably Hawkston would be marching westward, steadily cutting down the lead Gordon had had at the beginning.

But Gordon never had any doubt concerning his next move. He drank deep at the Well, and bolted some of the food the Arabs had been preparing for their breakfast. Some dried dates and crusted cheese-balls he placed in a food-bag, and he filled a water-skin from the Well. He retrieved his rifle, got the sand out of his automatic and buckled to his belt a scimitar from the girdle of one of the men he had killed. He had come into the desert intending to run and hide, not to fight. But it looked very much as if he would do much more fighting before this venture was over, and the added weight of the sword was more than balanced by the feeling of added security in the touch of the lean curved blade.

Then he slung the water-skin and food-bag over his shoulders, took up his rifle and strode out of the shadows of the grove into the molten heat of the desert day. He had not slept at all the night before. His short rest at the Well had put new life and spring into his resilient muscles, hardened and toughened by an incredibly strenuous life. But it was a long, long march to the Caves of El Khour, under a searing sun. Unless some miracle occurred, he could not hope to reach them before Hawkston now. And before another sun-rise the riders of Shalan ibn Mansour might well be on his trail, in which case—but all he had ever asked of Fortune was a fighting chance.

The sun rocked its slow, torturing way up the sky and down; twilight deepened into dusk, and the desert stars winked out; and on, grimly on, plodded that solitary figure, pitting an indomitable will against the merciless immensity of thirst-haunted desolation.

CHAPTER 4.

The Djinn of the Caves

THE CAVES OF EL KHOUR pit the sheer eastern walls of a gaunt hill-range that rises like a stony backbone out of a waste of rocky plains. There is only one spring in the hills; it rises in a cave high up in the wall and curls down the steep rocky slope, a slender thread of silver, to empty into a broad shallow pool below. The sun was hanging like a blood-red ball above the western desert when Francis Xavier Gordon halted near this pool and scanned the rows of gaping cave-mouths with blood-shot eyes. He licked heat-blackened lips with a tongue from which all moisture had been baked. Yet there was still a little water in the skin on his shoulder. He had economized on that gruelling march, with the savage economy of the wilderness-bred.

It seemed a bit hard to realize he had actually reached his goal. The hills of El Khour had shimmered before him for so many miles, unreal in the heat-waves, until at last they had seemed like a mirage, a fantasy of a thirst-maddened imagination. The desert sun plays tricks even with a brain like Gordon's. Slowly, slowly the hills had grown up before him—now he stood at the foot of the eastern-most cliff, frowning up at the tiers of caves which showed their black mouths in even rows.

Nightfall had not brought Shalan ibn Mansour's riders swooping after the solitary wanderer, nor had dawn brought them. Again and again through the long, hot day, Gordon had halted on some rise and looked back, expecting to see the dust of the hurrying camels; but the desert had stretched empty to the horizon.

And now it seemed another miracle had taken place, for there were no signs of Hawkston and his caravan. Had they come and gone? They would have at least watered their camels at the pool; and from the utter lack of signs about it, Gordon knew that no one had camped or watered animals at the pool for many moons. No, it was indisputable, even if unexplainable. Something had delayed Hawkston and Gordon had reached the Caves ahead of him after all.

The American dropped on his belly at the pool and sank his face into the cool water. He lifted his head presently, shook it like a lion shaking his mane, and leisurely washed the dust from his face and hands.

Then he rose and went toward the cliff. He had seen no sign of life, yet he knew that in one of those caves lived the man he had come to seek. He lifted his voice in a far-carrying shout.

"Al Wazir! Ho there, Al Wazir!"

"Wazirrr!" whispered the echo back from the cliff. There was no other answer. The silence was ominous. With his rifle at the ready Gordon went toward the narrow trail that wound up the rugged face of the cliff. Up this he climbed, keenly scanning the caves. They pitted the whole wall, in even tiers—too even to be the chance work of nature. They were man-made. Thousands of years ago, in the dim dawn of pre-history they had served as dwelling-places for some race of people who were not mere savages, who nitched their caverns in the soft strata with skill and cunning. Gordon knew the caves were connected by narrow passages, and that only by this ladder-like path he was following could they be reached from below.

The path ended at a long ledge, upon which all the caves of the lower tier opened. In the largest of these Al Wazir had taken up his abode.

Gordon called again, without result. He strode into the cave, and there he halted. It was square in shape. In the back wall and in each side wall showed a narrow door-like opening. Those at the sides led into adjoining caves. That at the back let into a smaller cavern, without any other outlet. There, Gordon remembered, Al Wazir had stored the dried and tinned foods he had brought with him. He had brought no furniture, nor weapons.

In one corner of the square cave a heap of charred fragments indicated that a fire had once been built there. In one corner lay a heap of skins—Al Wazir's bed. Nearby lay the one book Al Wazir had brought with him—*The Bhagavat-Gita*. But of the man himself there was no evidence.

Gordon went into the storeroom, struck a match and looked about him. The tins of food were there, though the supply was considerably depleted. But they were not stacked against the wall in neat columns as Gordon had seen them stowed under Al Wazir's directions. They were tumbled and scattered about all over the floor, with open and empty tins among them. This was not like Al Wazir, who placed a high value on neatness and order, even in small things. The rope he had brought along to aid him in exploring the caves lay coiled in one corner.

Gordon, extremely puzzled, returned to the square cave. Here, he had fully expected to find Al Wazir sitting in tranquil meditation, or out on the ledge meditating over the sun-set desert. Where was the man?

He was certain that Al Wazir had not wandered away to perish in the desert. There was no reason for him to leave the caves. If he had simply tired of his lonely life and taken his departure, he would have taken the book that was lying on the floor, his inseparable companion. There was no blood-stain on the floor, or anything to indicate that the hermit had met a violent end. Nor did Gordon believe that any Arab, even the Ruweila, would molest the "holy man." Anyway, if Arabs *had* done away with Al Wazir, they would have taken away the rope and the tins of food. And he was certain that, until Hawkston learned of it, no white man but himself had known of Al Wazir's whereabouts.

He searched through the lower tiers of caves without avail. The sun had sunk out of sight behind the hills, whose long shadows streamed far eastward across the desert, and deepening shadows filled the caverns. The silence and the mystery began to weigh on Gordon's nerves. He began to be irked by the feeling that unseen eyes were watching him. Men who live lives of constant peril develop certain obscure faculties or instincts to a keenness unknown to those lapped about by the securities of "civilization." As he passed through the caves, Gordon repeatedly felt an impulse to turn suddenly, to try to surprise those eyes that seemed to be boring into his back. At last he did wheel suddenly, thumb pressing back the hammer of his rifle, eyes alert for any movement in the growing dusk. The shadowy chambers and passages stood empty before him.

Once, as he passed a dark passageway he could have sworn he heard a soft noise, like the stealthy tread of a bare, furtive foot. He stepped to the mouth of the tunnel and called, without conviction: "Is that you, Ivan?" He shivered at the silence which followed; he had not really believed it was Al Wazir. He groped his way into the tunnel, rifle poked ahead of him. Within a few yards he encountered a blank wall; there seemed to be no entrance or exit except the doorway through which he had come. And the tunnel was empty, save for himself.

He returned to the ledge before the caves, in disgust.

"Hell, am I getting jumpy?"

But a grisly thought kept recurring to him—recollection of the Bedouins' belief that a supernatural fiend lurked in these ancient caves and devoured any human foolish enough to be caught there by night. This

thought kept recurring, together with the reflection that
the Orient held many secrets, which the West would laugh
at, but which often proved to be grim realities. That
would explain Al Wazir's mysterious absence: if some
fiendish or bestial dweller in the caves had devoured
him—Gordon's speculations revolved about a hypotheti-
cal rock-python of enormous size, dwelling for generations, perhaps centuries, in the hills—that would explain
the lack of any blood-stains. Abruptly he swore: "Damn!
I'm going batty. There are no snakes like that in Arabia.
These caves are getting on my nerves."

It was a fact. There was a brooding weirdness about
these ancient and forgotten caverns that roused uncanny
speculations in Gordon's predominantly Celtic mind.
What race had occupied them, so long ago? What wars
had they witnessed, against what fierce barbarians
sweeping up from the south? What cruelties and intrigues
had they known, what grim rituals of worship and human
sacrifice? Gordon shrugged his shoulders, wishing he had
not thought of human sacrifice. The idea fitted too well
with the general atmosphere of these grim caverns.

Angry at himself, he returned to the big square cavern,
which, he remembered, the Arabs called *Niss'rosh*, The
Eagle's Nest, for some reason or other. He meant to sleep
in the caves that night, partly to overcome the aversion he
felt toward them, partly because he did not care to be
caught down on the plain in case Hawkston or Shalan ibn
Mansour arrived in the night. There was another mystery.
Why had not they reached the Caves, one or both of
them? The desert was a breeding-place of mysteries, a
twilight realm of fantasy. Al Wazir, Hawkston and
Shalan ibn Mansour—had the fabled *djinn* of the Empty
Abodes snatched them up and flown away with them,
leaving him the one man alive in all the vast desert? Such
whims of imagination played through his exhausted
brain, as, too weary to eat, he prepared for the night.

He put a large rock in the trail, poised precariously,
which anyone climbing the path in the dark would be sure
to dislodge. The noise would awaken him. He stretched

himself on the pile of skins, painfully aware of the stress and strain of his long trek, which had taxed even his iron frame to the utmost. He was asleep almost the instant he touched his rude bed.

It was because of this weariness of body and mind that he did not hear the velvet-footed approach of the thing that crept upon him in the darkness. He woke only when taloned fingers clenched murderously on his throat and an inhuman voice whinnied sickening triumph in his ear.

Gordon's reflexes had been trained in a thousand battles. So now he was fighting for his life before he was awake enough to know whether it was an ape or a great serpent that had attacked him. The fierce fingers had almost crushed his throat before he had a chance to tense his neck muscles. Yet those powerful muscles, even though relaxed, had saved his life. Even so the attack was so stunning, the grasp so nearly fatal, that as they rolled over the floor Gordon wasted precious seconds trying to tear away the strangling hands by wrenching at the wrists. Then as his fighting brain asserted itself, even through the red, thickening mists that were enfolding him, he shifted his tactics, drove a savage knee into a hard-muscled belly, and getting his thumbs under the little finger of each crushing hand, bent them fiercely back. No strength can resist that leverage. The unknown attacker let go, and instantly Gordon smashed a trip-hammer blow against the side of his head and rolled clear as the hard frame went momentarily limp. It was as dark in the cave as the gullet of Hell, so dark Gordon could not even see his antagonist.

He sprang to his feet, drawing his scimitar. He stood poised, tense, wondering uncomfortably if the thing could see in the dark, and scarcely breathing as he strained his ears. At the first faint sound he sprang like a panther, and slashed murderously at the noise. The blade cut only empty air, there was an incoherent cry, a shuffle of feet, then the rapidly receding pad of hurried footsteps. Whatever it was, it was in retreat. Gordon tried to follow it, ran into a blank wall, and by the time he had located the side door through which, apparently, the creature had fled, the sounds had faded out. The American struck a match and glared around, not expecting to see anything that would give him a clue to the mystery. Nor did he. The rock floor of the cavern showed no footprint.

What manner of creature he had fought in the dark he did not know. Its body had not seemed hairy enough for an ape, though the head had been a tangled mass of hair. Yet it had not fought like a human being; he had felt its talons and teeth, and it was hard to believe that human muscles could have contained such iron strength as he had encountered. And the noises it had made had certainly not resembled the sounds a man makes, even in combat.

Gordon picked up his rifle and went out on the ledge. From the position of the stars, it was past midnight. He sat down on the ledge, with his back against the cliff wall. He did not intend to sleep, but he slept in spite of himself, and woke suddenly, to find himself on his feet, with every nerve tingling, and his skin crawling with the sensation that grim peril had crept close upon him.

Even as he wondered if a bad dream had awakened him, he glimpsed a vague shadow fading into the black mouth of a cave not far away. He threw up his rifle and the shot sent the echoes flying and ringing from cliff to cliff. He waited tensely, but neither saw nor heard anything else.

After that he sat with his rifle across his knees, every faculty alert. His position, he realized, was precarious. He was like a man marooned on a deserted island. It was a day's hard ride to the caravan road to the south. On foot it would take longer. He could reach it, unhindered—but unless Hawkston had abandoned the quest, which was not likely, the Englishman's caravan was moving along that road somewhere. If Gordon met it, alone and on foot—Gordon had no illusions about Hawkston. But there was still a greater danger: Shalan ibn Mansour. He did not know why the *shaykh* had not tracked him down already, but it was certain that Shalan, scouring the desert to find the man who slew his warriors at the Well of Amir Khan, would eventually run him down. When that happened, Gordon did not wish to be caught out on the desert, on foot. Here, in the Caves, with water, food and shelter, he would have at least a fighting chance. If Hawkston and Shalan should chance to arrive at the same time—that offered possibilities. Gordon was a fighting man who depended on his wits as much as his sword, and he had set his enemies tearing at each other before now. But there was a present menace to him, in the Caves themselves, a menace he felt was the solution to the riddle of Al Wazir's fate. That menace he meant to drive to bay with the coming of daylight.

He sat there until dawn turned the eastern sky rose and white. With the coming of the light he strained his eyes into the desert, expecting to see a moving line of dots that would mean men on camels. But only the tawny, empty waste levels and ridges met his gaze. Not until the sun was rising did he enter the caves; the level beams struck into them, disclosing features that had been veiled in shadows the evening before.

He went first to the passage where he had first heard the sinister footfalls, and there he found the explanation to one mystery. A series of hand and foot holds, lightly nitched in the stone of the wall, led up through a square hole in the rocky ceiling into the cave above. The *djinn* of the Caves had been in that passage, and had escaped by that route, for some reason choosing flight rather than battle just then.

Now that he was rested, he became aware of the bite of hunger, and headed for The Eagle's Nest, to get his breakfast out of the tins before he pursued his exploration of the caves. He entered the wide chamber, lighted by the early sun which streamed through the door—and stopped dead.

A bent figure in the door of the store-room wheeled erect, to face him. For an instant they both stood frozen. Gordon saw a man confronting him like an image of the primordial—naked, gaunt, with a great matted tangle of hair and beard, from which the eyes blazed weirdly. It might have been a caveman out of the dawn centuries who stood there, a stone gripped in each brawny hand. But the high, broad forehead, half hidden under the thatch of hair, was not the slanting brow of a savage. Nor was the face, almost covered though it was by the tangled beard.

"*Ivan!*" ejaculated Gordon aghast, and the explanation of the mystery rushed upon him, with all its sickening implications. Al Wazir was a madman.

As if goaded by the sound of his voice, the naked man started violently, cried out incoherently, and hurled the rock in his right hand. Gordon dodged and it shattered on the wall behind him with an impact that warned him of the unnatural power lurking in the maniac's thews. Al Wazir was taller than Gordon, with a magnificent, broad-shouldered, lean-hipped torso, ridged with muscles. Gordon half turned and set his rifle against the wall, and as he did so, Al Wazir hurled the rock in his left hand, awkwardly, and followed it across the cave with a bound, shrieking frightfully, foam flying from his lips.

Gordon met him breast to breast, bracing his muscular legs against the impact, and Al Wazir grunted explosively as he was stopped dead in his tracks. Gordon pinioned his arms at his side, and a wild shriek broke from the madman's lips as he tore and plunged like a trapped animal. His muscles were like quivering steel wires under Gordon's grasp, that writhed and knotted. His teeth snapped beast-like at Gordon's throat, and as the American jerked back his head to escape them, Al Wazir tore loose his right arm, and whipped it over Gordon's left arm and down. Before the American could prevent it, he had grasped the scimitar hilt and torn the blade from its scabbard. Up and back went the long arm, with the sheen of naked steel, and Gordon, sensing death in the lifted sword, smashed his left fist to the madman's jaw. It was a short terrific hook that traveled little more than a foot, but it was like the jolt of a mule's kick.

Al Wazir's head snapped back between his shoulders under the impact, then fell limply forward on his breast. His legs gave way simultaneously and Gordon caught him and eased him to the rocky floor.

Leaving the limp form where it lay, Gordon went hurriedly into the store-room and secured the rope. Returning to the senseless man he knotted it about his waist, then lifted him to a sitting position against a natural stone pillar at the back of the cave, passed the rope about the column and tied it with an intricate knot on the other side. The rope was too strong, even for the superhuman strength of a maniac, and Al Wazir could not reach backward around the pillar to reach and untie the knot. Then Gordon set to work reviving the man—no light task, for El Borak, with the peril of death upon him, had struck hard, with the drive and snap of steel-trap muscles. Only the heavy beard had saved the jaw-bone from fracture.

But presently the eyes opened and gazed wildly around, flaring redly as they fixed on Gordon's face. The clawing hands with their long black nails, came up and caught at Gordon's throat, as the American drew back out of reach. Al Wazir made a convulsive effort to rise, then sank back and crouched, with his unwinking stare, his fingers making aimless motions. Gordon looked at him somberly, sick at his soul. What a miserable, revolting end to dreams and philosophies! Al Wazir had come into the desert seeking meditation and peace and the visions of the ancient prophets; he had found horror and insanity. Gordon had come looking for a hermit-philosopher, radiant with mellow wisdom; he had found a filthy, naked madman.

The American filled an empty tin with water and set it, with an opened tin of meat, near Al Wazir's hand. An instant later he dodged, as the mad hermit hurled the tins at him with all his power. Shaking his head in despair, Gordon went into the store-room and broke his own fast. He had little heart to eat, with the ruin of that once-splendid personality before him, but the urgings of hunger would not be denied.

It was while thus employed that a sudden noise outside brought him to his feet, galvanized by the imminence of danger.

CHAPTER 5.

Hawks at Bay

IT WAS THE rattling fall of the stone Gordon had placed in the path that had alarmed him. Someone was climbing up the winding trail! Snatching up his rifle he glided out on the ledge. One of his enemies had come at last.

Down at the pool a weary, dusty camel was drinking. On the path, a few feet below the ledge there stood a tall, wiry man in dust-stained boots and breeches, his torn shirt revealing his brown, muscular chest.

"Gordon!" this man ejaculated, staring amazedly into the black muzzle of the American's rifle. "How the devil did you get here?" His hands were empty, resting on an outcropping of rock, just as he had halted in the act of climbing. His rifle was slung to his back, pistol and scimitar in their scabbards at his belt.

"Put up your hands, Hawkston," ordered Gordon, and the Englishman obeyed.

"What are you doing here?" he repeated. "I left you in el-Azem—"

"Salim lived long enough to tell me what he saw in the hut by Mekmet's Pool. I came by a road you know nothing about. Where are the other jackals?"

Hawkston shook the sweat-beads from his sun-burnt forehead. He was above medium height, brown, hard as sole-leather, with a dark hawk-like face and a high-bridged predatory nose arching over a thin black mustache. A lawless adventurer, his scintillant grey eyes reflected a ruthless and reckless nature, and as a fighting man he was as notorious as was Gordon—more notorious in Arabia, for Afghanistan had been the stage for most of El Borak's exploits.

"My men? Dead by now, I fancy. The Ruweila are on the war-path. Shalan ibn Mansour caught us at Sulaymen's Well, with fifty men. We made a barricade of our saddles among the palms and stood them off all day. Van Brock and three of our camel-drivers were killed during the fighting, and Krakovitch was wounded. That night I took a camel and cleared out. I knew it was no use hanging on."

"You swine," said Gordon without passion. He did not call Hawkston a coward. He knew that not cowardice, but a cynical determination to save his skin at all hazards had driven the Englishman to desert his wounded and beleaguered companions.

"There wasn't any use for us all to be killed," retorted Hawkston. "I believed one man could sneak away in the dark and I did. They rushed the camp just as I got clear. I heard them killing the others. Ortelli howled like a lost soul when they cut his throat—I knew they'd run me down long before I could reach the Coast, so I headed for the Caves—northwest across the open desert, leaving the road and Khosru's Well off to the south. It was a long, dry ride, and I made it more by luck than anything else. And now can I put my hands down?"

"You might as well," replied Gordon, the rifle at his shoulder never wavering. "In a few seconds it won't matter much to you where your hands are."

Hawkston's expression did not change. He lowered his hands, but kept them away from his belt.

"You mean to kill me?" he asked calmly.

"You murdered my friend Salim. You came here to

torture and rob Al Wazir. You'd kill me if you got the chance. I'd be a fool to let you live."

"Are you going to shoot me in cold blood?"

"No. Climb up on the ledge. I'll give you any kind of an even break you want."

Hawkston complied, and a few seconds later stood facing the American. An observer would have been struck by a certain similarity between the two men. There was no facial resemblance, but both were burned dark by the sun, both were built with the hard economy of rawhide and spring steel, and both wore the keen, hawk-like aspect which is the common brand of men who live by their wits and guts out on the raw edges of the world.

Hawkston stood with his empty hands at his sides while Gordon faced him with rifle held hip-low, but covering his midriff.

"Rifles, pistols or swords?" asked the American. "They say you can handle a blade."

"Second to none in Arabia," answered Hawkston confidently. "But I'm not going to fight you, Gordon."

"You will!" A red flame began to smolder in the black eyes. "I know you, Hawkston. You've got a slick tongue, and you're treacherous as a snake. We'll settle this thing here and now. Choose your weapons—or by God, I'll shoot you down in your tracks!"

Hawkston shook his head calmly.

"You wouldn't shoot a man in cold blood, Gordon. I'm not going to fight you—yet. Listen, man, we'll have plenty of fighting on our hands before long! Where's Al Wazir?"

"That's none of your business," growled Gordon.

"Well, no matter. You know why I'm here. And I know you came here to stop me if you could. But just now you and I are in the same boat. Shalan ibn Mansour's on my trail. I slipped through his fingers, as I said, but he picked up my tracks and was after me within a matter of hours. His camels were faster and fresher than mine, and he's been slowly overhauling me. When I topped the tallest of those ridges to the south there, I saw his dust. He'll be here within the next hour! He hates you as much as he does me.

You need my help, and I need yours. With Al Wazir to help us, we can hold these Caves indefinitely."

Gordon frowned. Hawkston's tale sounded plausible, and would explain why Shalan ibn Mansour had not come hot on the American's trail, and why the Englishman had not arrived at the Caves sooner. But Hawkston was such a snake-tongued liar it was dangerous to trust him. The merciless creed of the desert said shoot him down without any more parley, and take his camel. Rested, it would carry Gordon and Al Wazir out of the desert. But Hawkston had gauged Gordon's character correctly when he said the American could not shoot a man in cold blood.

"Don't move," Gordon warned him, and holding the cocked rifle like a pistol in one hand, he disarmed Hawkston, and ran a hand over him to see that he had no concealed weapons. If his scruples prevented him shooting his enemy, he was determined not to give that enemy a chance to get the drop on him. For he knew Hawkston had no such scruples.

"How do I know you're not lying?" he demanded.

"Would I have come here alone, on a worn-out camel, if I wasn't telling the truth?" countered Hawkston. "We'd better hide that camel, if we can. If we should beat them off, we'll need it to get to the Coast on. Damn it, Gordon, your suspicion and hesitation will get our throats cut yet! Where's Al Wazir?"

"Turn and look into that cave," replied Gordon grimly.

Hawkston, his face suddenly sharp with suspicion, obeyed. As his eyes rested on the figure crouched against the column at the back of the cavern, his breath sucked in sharply.

"Al Wazir! What in God's name's the matter with him?"

"Too much loneliness, I reckon," growled Gordon. "He's stark mad. He couldn't tell you where to find the Blood of the Gods if you tortured him all day."

"Well, it doesn't matter much just now," muttered Hawkston callously. "Can't think of treasure when life itself is at stake. Gordon, you'd better believe me! We should be preparing for a siege, not standing here chinning. If Shalan ibn Mansour—*look!*" He started violently, his long arm stabbing toward the south.

Gordon did not turn at the exclamation. He stepped back instead, out of the Englishman's reach, and still covering the man, shifted his position so he could watch both Hawkston and the point of the compass indicated. Southeastward the country was undulating, broken by barren ridges. Over the farthest ridge a string of white dots was pouring, and a faint dust-haze billowed up in the air. Men on camels! A regular horde of them.

"The Ruweila!" exclaimed Hawkston. "They'll be here within the hour!"

"They may be men of yours," answered Gordon, too wary to accept anything not fully proven. Hawkston was as tricky as a fox, and to make a mistake on the desert meant death. "We'll hide that camel, though, just on the chance you're telling the truth. Go ahead of me down the trail."

Paying no attention to the Englishman's profanity, Gordon herded him down the path to the pool. Hawkston took the camel's rope and went ahead leading it, under Gordon's guidance. A few hundred yards north of the pool there was a narrow canyon winding deep into a break of the hills, and a short distance up this ravine Gordon showed Hawkston a narrow cleft in the wall, concealed behind a jutting boulder. Through this the camel was squeezed, into a natural pocket, open at the top, roughly round in shape, and about forty feet across.

"I don't know whether the Arabs know about this place or not," said Gordon. "But we'll have to take the chance that they won't find the beast."

Hawkston was nervous.

"For God's sake let's get back to the Caves! They're coming like the wind. If they catch us in the open they'll shoot us like rabbits!"

He started back at a run, and Gordon was close on his heels. But Hawkston's nervousness was justified. The

white men had not quite reached the foot of the trail that
led up to the Caves when a low thunder of hoofs rose on
their ears, and over the nearest ridge came a wild white-
clad figure on a camel, waving a rifle. At the sight of them
he yelled stridently and flogged his beast into a more
furious gallop, and threw his rifle to his shoulder. Behind
him man after man topped the ridge—Bedouins on
hejin—white racing camels.

"Up the cliff, man!" yelled Hawkston, pale under his
bronze. Gordon was already racing up the path, and
behind him Hawkston panted and cursed, urging greater
haste, where more speed was impossible. Bullets began to
snick against the cliff, and the foremost rider howled in
blood-thirsty glee as he bore down swiftly upon them. He
was many yards ahead of his companions, and he was a
remarkable marksman, for an Arab. Firing from the
rocking, swaying saddle, he was clipping his targets close.

Hawkston yelped as he was stung by a flying sliver of
rock, flaked off by a smashing slug.

"Damn you, Gordon!" he panted. "This is your fault—
your bloody stubbornness—he'll pick us off like rabbits—"

The oncoming rider was not more than three hundred
yards from the foot of the cliff, and the rim of the ledge
was ten feet above the climbers. Gordon wheeled
suddenly, threw his rifle to his shoulder and fired all in
one motion, so quickly he did not even seem to take aim.
But the Arab went out of his saddle like a man hit by
lightning. Without pausing to note the result of his shot,
Gordon raced on up the path, and an instant later he
swarmed over the ledge, with Hawkston at his heels.

"Damndest snap-shot I ever saw!" gasped the Englishman.

"There's your guns," grunted Gordon, throwing
himself flat on the ledge. "Here they come!"

Hawkston snatched his weapons from the rock where
Gordon had left them, and followed the American's
example.

The Arabs had not paused. They greeted the fall of

their reckless leader with yells of hate, but they flogged their mounts and came on in a headlong rush. They meant to spring off at the foot of the trail and charge up it on foot. There were at least fifty of them.

The two men lying prone on the ledge above did not lose their heads. Veterans, both of them, of a thousand wild battles, they waited coolly until the first of the riders were within good range. Then they began firing, without haste and without error. And at each shot a man tumbled headlong from his saddle or slumped forward on his mount's bobbing neck.

Not even Bedouins could charge into such a blast of destruction. The rush wavered, split, turned on itself—and in an instant the white-clad riders were turning their backs on the Caves and flogging in the other direction as madly as they had come. Five of them would never charge again, and as they fled Hawkston drilled one of the rear-most men neatly between the shoulders.

They fell back beyond the first low, stone-littered ridge, and Hawkston shook his rifle at them and cursed them with virile eloquence.

"Desert scum! Try it again, you bounders!"

Gordon wasted no breath on words. Hawkston had told the truth, and Gordon knew he was in no danger from treachery from that source, for the present. Hawkston would not attack him as long as they were confronted by a common enemy—but he knew that the instant that peril was removed, the Englishman might shoot him in the back, if he could. Their position was bad, but it might well have been worse. The Bedouins were all seasoned desert-fighters, cruel as wolves. Their chief had a blood-feud with both white men, and would not fail to grasp the chance that had thrown them into his reach. But the defenders had the advantage of shelter, an inexhaustible water supply, and food enough to last for months. Their only weakness was the limited amount of ammunition.

Without consulting one another, they took their stations on the ledge, Hawkston to the north of the trail-head, Gordon about an equal distance to the south of it.

There was no need for a conference; each man knew the other knew his business. They lay prone, gathering broken rocks in heaps before them to add to the protection offered by the ledge-rim.

Spurts of flame began to crown the ridge; bullets whined and splatted against the rock. Men crept from each end of the ridge into the clusters of boulders that littered the plain. The men on the ledge held their fire, unmoved by the slugs that whistled and spanged near at hand. Their minds worked so similarly in a situation like this that they understood each other without the necessity of conversation. There was no chance of them wasting two cartridges on the same man. An imaginary line, running from the foot of the trail to the ridge, divided their territories. When a turbaned head was poked from a rock north of that line, it was Hawkston's rifle that knocked the man dead and sprawling over the boulder. And when a Bedouin darted from behind a spur of rock south of that line in a weaving, dodging run for cover nearer the cliff, Hawkston held his fire. Gordon's rifle cracked and the runner took the earth in a rolling tumble that ended in a brief thrashing of limbs.

A voice rose from the ridge, edged with fury.

"That's Shalan, damn him!" snarled Hawkston. "Can you make out what he says?"

"He's telling his men to keep out of sight," answered Gordon. "He tells them to be patient—they've got plenty of time."

"And that's the truth, too," grunted Hawkston. "They've got time, food, water—they'll be sneaking to the pool after dark to fill their water-skins. I wish one of us could get a clean shot at Shalan. But he's too foxy to give us a chance at him. I saw him when they were charging us, standing back on the ridge, too far away to risk a bullet on him."

"If we could drop him the rest of them wouldn't hang around here a minute," commented Gordon. "They're afraid of the man-eating *djinn* they think haunts these hills."

"Well, if they could get a good look at Al Wazir now,

they'd swear it was the *djinn* in person," said Hawkston. "How many cartridges have you?"

"Both guns are full, about a dozen extra rifle cartridges."

Hawkston swore.

"I haven't many more than that, myself. We'd better toss a coin to see which one of us sneaks out tonight, while the other keeps up a fusilade to distract their attention. The one who stays gets both rifles and all the ammunition."

"We will like hell," growled Gordon. "If we can't all go, Al Wazir with us, nobody goes!"

"You're crazy to think of a lunatic at a time like this!"

"Maybe. But if you try to sneak off I'll drill you in the back as you run."

Hawkston snarled wordlessly and fell silent. Both men lay motionless as red Indians, watching the ridge and the rocks that shimmered in the heat waves. The firing had ceased, but they had glimpses of white garments from time to time among the gullies and stones, as the besiegers crept about among the boulders. Some distance to the south Gordon saw a group creeping along a shallow gully that ran to the foot of the cliff. He did not waste lead on them. When they reached the cliff at that point they would be no better off. They were too far away for effective shooting, and the cliff could be climbed only at the point where the trail wound upward. Gordon fell to studying the hill that was serving the white men as their fortress.

Some thirty caves formed the lower tier, extending across the curtain of rock that formed the face of the cliff. As he knew, each cave was connected by a narrow passage to the adjoining chamber. There were three tiers above this one, all the tiers connected by ladders of hand-holds nitched in the rock, mounting from the lower caves through holes in the stone ceiling to the ones above. The Eagle's Nest, in which Al Wazir was tied, safe from flying lead, was approximately in the middle of the lower tier, and the path hewn in the rock came upon the ledge directly before its opening. Hawkston was lying in front of the third cave to the north of it, and Gordon lay before the third cave to the south.

The Arabs lay in a wide semi-circle, extending from the rocks at one end of the low ridge, along its crest, and into the rocks at the other end. Only those lying among the rocks were close enough to do any damage, save by accident. And looking up at the ledge from below, they could see only the gleaming muzzles of the white men's rifles, or catch fleeting glimpses of their heads occasionally. They seemed to be weary of wasting lead on such difficult targets. Not a shot had been fired for some time.

Gordon found himself wondering if a man on the crest of the cliff above the caves could, looking down, see him and Hawkston lying on the ledge. He studied the wall above him; it was almost sheer, but other, narrower ledges ran along each tier of caves, obstructing the view from above, as it did from the lower ledge. Remembering the craggy sides of the hill, Gordon did not believe these plains-dwellers would be able to scale it at any point.

He was just contemplating returning to The Eagle's Nest to offer food and water again to Al Wazir, when a faint sound reached his ears that caused him to go tense with suspicion.

It seemed to come from the caves behind him. He glanced at Hawkston. The Englishman was squinting along his rifle barrel, trying to get a bead on a *kafieh* that kept bobbing in and out among the boulders near the end of the ridge.

Gordon wriggled back from the ledge-rim and rolled into the mouth of the nearest cave before he stood up, out of sight of the men below. He stood still, straining his ears.

There it was again—soft and furtive, like the rustle of cloth against stone, the shuffle of bare feet. It came from some point south of where he stood. Gordon moved silently in that direction, passed through the adjoining chamber, entered the next—and came face to face with a tall beared Bedouin who yelled and whirled up a scimitar. Another raider, a man with an evil, scarred face, was directly behind him, and three more were crawling out of a cleft in the floor.

Gordon fired from the hip, checking the downward stroke of the scimitar. The scar-faced Arab fired over the falling body and Gordon felt a numbing shock run up his arms, jerked the trigger and got no response. The bullet had smashed into the lock, ruining the mechanism. He heard Hawkston yell savagely, out on the ledge, heard the pumping fusilade of the Englishman's rifle, and a storm of shots and yells rising from the valley. They were storming the cliff! And Hawkston must meet them alone, for Gordon had his hands full.

What takes long to relate, actually happened in split seconds. Before the scarred Bedouin could fire again Gordon knocked him sprawling with a kick in the groin, and reversing his rifle, crushed the skull of a man who lunged at him with a long knife. No time to draw pistol or scimitar. It was hand-to-hand slaughter with a vengeance in the narrow cave, two Bedouins tearing at him like wolves, and others jamming the shaft in their eagerness to join the fray.

No quarter given or expected—a whirlwind of furious motion, blades flashing and whickering, clanging on the rifle barrel and biting into the stock as Gordon parried— and the butt crushing home and men going down with their heads smashed. The scarred nomad had risen, but fearing to fire because of the desperate closeness of the melee, rushed in, clubbing his rifle, just as the last man dropped. Gordon, bleeding from a gash across the breast muscles, ducked the swinging stock, shifted his grip on his own rifle and drove the blood-smeared butt, like a dagger, full in the bearded face. Teeth and bones crumpled and the man toppled backward into the shaft, carrying with him the men who were just clambering out.

Snatching the instant's respite Gordon sprang to the mouth of the shaft, whipping out his automatic. Wild bearded faces crowding the shaft glared up at him, frozen with the recognition of doom—then the cave reverberated deafeningly to the thundering of the big automatic, blasting those wild faces into red ruin. It was slaughter at that range, blood and brains spattered, nerveless hands released their holds, bodies went sliding down the shaft in a red welter, jamming and choking it.

Gordon glared down it for an instant, all killer in that moment, then whirled and ran out on the ledge. Bullets sang past his head, and he saw Hawkston stuffing fresh cartridges into his rifle. No living Arab was in sight, but half a dozen new forms between the ridge and the foot of the trail told of a determined effort to storm the cliff, defeated only by the Englishman's deadly accuracy.

Hawkston shouted: "What the hell's been going on in there?"

"They've found a shaft leading up from somewhere down below," snapped Gordon. "Watch for another rush while I try to jam it."

Ignoring lead slapped at him from among the rocks, he found a sizable boulder and rolled it into the cave. He peered cautiously down the well. Hand and foot holds nitched in the rock formed precarious stair-steps in the slanting side. Some forty feet down the shaft made an angle, and it was there the bodies of the Arabs had jammed. But now only one corpse hung there, and as he looked it moved, as if imbued with life, and slid down out of sight. Men below the angle were pulling the bodies out, to clear the way for a fresh attack.

Gordon rolled the boulder into the shaft and it rumbled downward and wedged hard at the angle. He did not believe it could be dislodged from below, and his belief was confirmed by a muffled chorus of maledictions swelling up from the depths.

Gordon was sure this shaft had not been in existence when he first came to the Caves with Al Wazir, a year before. Exploring the caverns in search of the madman, the night before, it was not strange that he had failed to notice the narrow mouth in a dark corner of the cave. That it opened into some cleft at the foot of the cliff was obvious. He remembered the men he had seen stealing along the gully to the south. They had found that lower cleft, and the simultaneous attack from both sides had been well planned. But for Gordon's keen ears it might have succeeded. As it was it had left the American with an empty pistol and a broken rifle.

Gordon dragged the bodies of the four Arabs he had killed to the ledge and heaved them over, ignoring the ferocious yells and shots that emanated from the rocks. He did not bother to marvel that he had emerged the victor from that desperate melee. He knew that fighting was half speed and strength and wit, and half blind luck. His number was not up yet, that was all.

Then he set out on a thorough tour of investigation through the lower tiers, in search of other possible shafts. Passing through The Eagle's Nest, he glanced at Al Wazir, sitting against the pillar. The man seemed to be asleep; his hairy head was sunk on his breast, his hands folded limply over the rope about his waist. Gordon set food and water beside him.

His explorations revealed no more unexpected tunnels. Gordon returned to the ledge with tins of food and a skin of water, procured from the stream which had its source in one of the caves. They ate lying flat on the shelf, for keen eyes were watching with murderous hate and eager trigger-finger from ridge and rock. The sun had passed its zenith.

Their frugal meal finished, the white men lay baking in the heat like lizards on a rock, watching the ridge. The afternoon waned.

"You've got another rifle," said Hawkston.

"Mine was broken in the fight in the cave. I took this one from one of the men I killed. It has a full magazine, but no more cartridges for it. My pistol's empty."

"I've got only the cartridges in my guns," muttered Hawkston. "Looks like our number's up. They're just waiting for dark before they rush us again. One of us might get away in the dark, while the other held the fort, but since you won't agree to that, there's nothing to do but sit here and wait until they cut our throats."

"We have one chance," said Gordon. "If we can kill

Shalan, the others will run. He's not afraid of man or devil, but his men fear *djinn*. They'll be nervous as the devil after night falls."

Hawkston laughed harshly. "Fool's talk. Shalan won't give us a chance at him. We'll all die here. All but Al Wazir. The Arabs won't harm him. But they won't help him, either. Damn him! Why did he have to go mad?"

"It wasn't very considerate," Gordon agreed with biting irony. "But then, you see he didn't know you wanted to torture him into telling where he hid the Blood of the Gods."

"It wouldn't have been the first time a man has been tortured for them," retorted Hawkston. "Man, you have no real idea of the value of those jewels. I saw them once, when Al Wazir was governor of Oman. The sight of them's enough to drive a man mad. Their story sounds like a tale out of *The Arabian Nights*. Only God knows how many women have given up their souls or men their lives because of them, since Ala ed-din Muhammad of Delhi plundered the Hindu temple of Somnath, and found them among the loot. That was in 1294. They've blazed a crimson path across Asia since then. Blood's spilt wherever they go. I'd poison my own brother to get them—" The wild flame that rose in the Englishman's eyes made it easy for Gordon to believe it, and he was swept by a revulsion toward the man.

"I'm going to feed Al Wazir," he said abruptly, rising.

No shots had come from the rocks for some time, though they knew their foes were there, waiting with their ancient, terrible patience. The sun had sunk behind the hills, the ravines and ridges were veiled in great blue shadows. Away to the east a silver-bright star winked out and quivered in the deepening blue.

Gordon strode into the square chamber—and was galvanized at the sight of the stone pillar standing empty. With a stride he reached it, bent over the frayed ends of the severed rope that told their own story. Al Wazir had found a way to free himself. Slowly, painfully, working with his claw-like fingernails through the long day, the madman had picked apart the tough strands of the heavy rope. And he was gone.

CHAPTER 6.

The Devil of the Night

GORDON STEPPED TO the door of the Nest and said curtly:
"Al Wazir's gotten away. I'm going to search the Caves
for him. Stay on the ledge and keep watch."

"Why waste the last minutes of your life chasing a
lunatic through a rat-run?" growled Hawkston. "It'll be
dark soon and the Arabs will be rushing us—"

"You wouldn't understand," snarled Gordon, turning
away.

The task ahead of him was distasteful. Searching for a
homicidal maniac through the darkening caves was bad
enough, but the thought of having forcibly to subdue his
friend again was revolting. But it must be done. Left to
run at large in the Caves Al Wazir might do harm either to
himself or to them. A stray bullet might strike him down.

A swift search through the lower tier proved fruitless,
and Gordon mounted by the ladder into the second tier.
As he climbed through the hole into the cave above he had
an uncomfortable feeling that Al Wazir was crouching at
the rim to break his head with a rock. But only silence and
emptiness greeted him. Dusk was filling the caves so

swiftly he began to despair of finding the madman. There were a hundred nooks and corners where Al Wazir could crouch unobserved, and Gordon's time was short.

The ladder that connected the second tier with the third was in the chamber into which he had come, and glancing up through it Gordon was startled to see a circle of deepening blue set with a winking star. In an instant he was climbing toward it.

He had discovered another unsuspected exit from the Caves. The ladder of hand holds led through the ceiling, up the wall of the cave above, and up through a round shaft that opened in the ceiling of the highest cave. He went up, like a man climbing up a chimney, and a few moments later thrust his head over the rim.

He had come out on the summit of the cliffs. To the east the rock rim pitched up sharply, obstructing his view, but to the west he looked out over a jagged backbone that broke in gaunt crags outlined against the twilight. He stiffened as somewhere a pebble rattled down, as if dislodged by a groping foot. Had Al Wazir come this way? Was the madman somewhere out there, climbing among those shadowy crags? If he was, he was courting death by the slip of a hand or a foot.

As he strained his eyes in the deepening shadows, a call welled up from below: "I say, Gordon! The blighters are getting ready to rush us! I see them massing among the rocks!"

With a curse Gordon started back down the shaft. It was all he could do. With darkness gathering Hawkston would not be able to hold the ledge alone.

Gordon went down swiftly, but before he reached the ledge darkness had fallen, lighted but little by the stars. The Englishman crouched on the rim, staring down into the dim gulf of shadows below.

"They're coming!" he muttered, cocking his rifle. "Listen!"

There was no shooting, this time—only the swift purposeful slap of sandalled feet over the stones. In the faint starlight a shadowy mass detached itself from the

outer darkness and rolled toward the foot of the cliff.
Steel clinked on the rocks. The mass divided into
individual figures. Men grew up out of the darkness
below. No use to waste bullets on shadows. The white
men held their fire. The Arabs were on the trail, and they
came up with a rush, steel gleaming dully in their hands.
The path was thronged with dim figures; the defenders
caught the glitter of white eyeballs, rolling upward.

They began to work their rifles. The dark was cut with
incessant spurts of flame. Lead thudded home. Men cried
out. Bodies rolled from the trail, to strike sickeningly on
the rocks below. Somewhere back in the darkness, Shalan
ibn Mansour's voice was urging on his slayers. The crafty
shaykh had no intentions of risking his hide within reach
of those grim fighters holding the ledge.

Hawkston cursed him as he worked his rifle.

"*Thibhahum, bism er rassul!*" sobbed the blood-
lusting howl as the maddened Bedouins fought their way
upward, frothing like rabid dogs in their hate and
eagerness to tear the Infidels limb from limb.

Gordon's hammer fell with an empty click. He clubbed
the rifle and stepped to the head of the path. A white-clad
form loomed before him, fighting for a foothold on the
ledge. The swinging rifle-butt crushed his head like an
egg-shell. A rifle fired point-blank singed Gordon's brows
and his gun-stock shattered the rifleman's shoulder.

Hawkston fired his last cartridge, hurled the empty
rifle and leaped to Gordon's side, scimitar in hand. He cut
down a Bedouin who was scrambling over the rim with a
knife in his teeth. The Arabs massed in a milling clump
below the rim, snarling like wolves, flinching from the
blows that rained down from rifle butt and scimitar.

Men began to slink back down the trail.

"*Wallah!*" wailed a man. "They are devils! Flee,
brothers!"

"Dogs!" yelled Shalan ibn Mansour, an eery voice out
of the darkness. He stood on a low knoll near the ridge,
but he was invisible to the men on the cliff, what of the
thick shadows. "Stand to it! There are but two of them!

They have ceased firing, so their guns must be empty! If you do not bring me their heads I will flay you alive! They—*ahhh*! *Ya allah*—!" His voice rose to an incoherent scream, and then broke in a horrible gurgle. That was followed by a tense silence, in which the Arabs clinging to the trail and massed at its foot twisted their heads over their shoulders to glare in amazement in the direction whence the cry had come. The men on the ledge, glad of the respite, shook the sweat from their eyes and stood listening with equal surprise and interest.

Someone called: "Ohai, Shalan ibn Mansour! Is all well with thee?"

There was no reply, and one of the Arabs left the foot of the cliff and ran toward the knoll, shouting the *shaykh*'s name. The men on the ledge could trace his progress by his strident voice.

"Why did the *shaykh* cry out and fall silent?" shouted a man on the path. "What has happened, Haditha?"

Haditha's reply came back plainly.

"I have reached the knoll whereon he stood—I do not see him—*Wallah*! He is dead! He lies here slain, with his throat torn out! Allah! *Help*!" He screamed, fired, and then came sounds of his frantic flight. And as he howled like a lost soul, for the flash of the shot had showed him a face stooping above the dead man, a wild grinning visage rendered inhuman by a matted tangle of hair—the face of a devil to the terrified Arab. And above his shrieks, as he ran, rose burst upon burst of maniacal laughter.

"Flee! Flee! I have seen it! It is the *djinn* of El Khour!"

Instant panic ensued. Men fell off the trail like ripe apples off a limb screaming: "The *djinn* has slain Shalan ibn Mansour! Flee, brothers, flee!" The night was filled with their clamor as they stampeded for the ridge, and presently the sounds of lusty whacking and the grunting of camels came back to the men on the ledge. There was no trick about this. The Ruweila, courageous in the face of human foes, but haunted by superstitious terrors, were in full flight, leaving behind them the bodies of their chief and their slain comrades.

"What the devil?" marveled Hawkston.

"It must have been Ivan," muttered Gordon. "Somehow he must have climbed down the crags on the other side of the hill—God, what a climb it must have been!"

They stood there listening, but the only sound that reached their ears was the diminishing noise of the horde's wild flight. Presently they descended the path, past forms grotesquely huddled where they had fallen. More bodies dotted the floor at the foot of the cliff, and Gordon picked up a rifle dropped from a dead hand, and assured himself that it was loaded. With the Arabs in flight, the truce between him and Hawkston might well be at an end. Their future relations would depend entirely upon the Englishman.

A few moments later they stood upon the low knoll on which Shalan ibn Mansour had stood. The Arab chief was still there. He sprawled on his back in a dark crimson puddle, and his throat had been ripped open as if by the claws of a wild beast. He was a grisly sight in the light of the match Gordon shaded over him.

The American straightened, blew out the match and flipped it away. He strained his eyes into the surrounding shadows and called: "Ivan!" There was no answer.

"Do you suppose it was really Al Wazir who killed him?" asked Hawkston uneasily.

"Who else could it have been? He must have sneaked on Shalan from behind. The other fellow caught a glimpse of him, and thought he was the devil of the caves, just as you said they would." What erratic whim had impelled Al Wazir to this deed, Gordon could not say. Who can guess the vagaries of the insane? The primitive instincts of murder loosed by lunacy—a madman stealing through the night, attracted by a solitary figure shouting from a knoll—it was not so strange, after all.

"Well, let's start looking for him," growled Hawkston. "I know you won't start back to the Coast until we've got him nicely tied up on that bally camel. So the sooner the better."

"All right." Gordon's voice betrayed none of the

suspicion in his mind. He knew that Hawkston's nature and purposes had been altered none by what they had passed through. The man was treacherous and unpredictable as a wolf. He turned and started toward the cliff, but he took good care not to let the Englishman get behind him, and he carried his cocked rifle ready.

"I want to find the lower end of that shaft the Arabs came up," said Gordon. "Ivan may be hiding there. It must be near the western end of that gully they were sneaking along when I first saw them."

Not long later they were moving along the shallow gully, and where it ended against the foot of the cliff, they saw a narrow slit-like cleft in the stone, large enough to admit a man. Hoarding their matches carefully they entered and moved along the narrow tunnel into which it opened. This tunnel led straight back into the cliff for a short distance, then turned sharply to the right, running along until it ended in a small chamber cut out of solid rock, which Gordon believed was directly under the room in which he had fought the Arabs. His belief was confirmed when they found the opening of the shaft leading upward. A match held up in the well showed the angle still blocked by the boulder.

"Well, we know how they got into the Caves," growled Hawkston. "But we haven't found Al Wazir. He's not in here."

"We'll go up into the Caves," answered Gordon. "He'll come back there for food. We'll catch him then."

"And then what?" demanded Hawkston.

"It's obvious, isn't it? We hit out for the caravan road. Ivan rides. We walk. We can make it, all right. I don't believe the Ruweila will stop before they get back to the tents of their tribe. I'm hoping Ivan's mind can be restored when we get him back to civilization."

"And what about the Blood of the Gods?"

"Well, what about them? They're his, to do what he pleases with them."

Hawkston did not reply, nor did he seem aware of

Gordon's suspicion of him. He had no rifle, but Gordon knew the pistol at his hip was loaded. The American carried his rifle in the crook of his arm, and he maneuvered so the Englishman went ahead of him as they groped their way back down the tunnel and out into the starlight. Just what Hawkston's intentions were, he did not know. Sooner or later, he believed, he would have to fight the Englishman for his life. But somehow he felt that this would not be necessary until after Al Wazir had been found and secured.

He wondered about the tunnel and the shaft to the top of the cliff. They had not been there a year ago. Obviously the Arabs had found the tunnel purely by accident.

"No use searching the Caves tonight," said Hawkston, when they had reached the ledge. "We'll take turns watching and sleeping. Take the first watch, will you? I didn't sleep last night, you know."

Gordon nodded. Hawkston dragged the sleeping-skins from the Nest and wrapping himself in them, fell asleep close to the wall. Gordon sat down a short distance away, his rifle across his knees. As he sat he dozed lightly, waking each time the sleeping Englishman stirred.

He was still sitting there when the dawn reddened the eastern sky.

Hawkston rose, stretched and yawned.

"Why didn't you wake me to watch my turn?" he asked.

"You know damned well why I didn't," grated Gordon. "I don't care to run the risk of being murdered in my sleep."

"You don't like me, do you, Gordon?" laughed Hawkston. But only his lips smiled, and a red flame smoldered in his eyes. "Well, that makes the feeling mutual, don't you know. After we've gotten Al Wazir back to el-Azem, I'm looking forward to a gentlemanly settling of our differences—just you and I—and a pair of swords."

"Why wait until then?" Gordon was on his feet, his nostrils quivering with the eagerness of hard-leashed hate.

Hawkston shook his head, smiling fiercely.

"Oh no, El Borak. No fighting until we get out of the desert."

"All right," snarled the American disgruntledly. "Let's eat, and then start combing the Caves for Ivan."

A slight sound brought them both wheeling toward the door of the Nest. Al Wazir stood there, plucking at his beard with his long black nails. His eyes lacked their former wild beast glare; they were clouded, plaintive. His attitude was one of bewilderment rather than menace.

"Ivan!" muttered Gordon, setting down his rifle and moving toward the wild man. Al Wazir did not retreat, nor did he make any hostile demonstration. He stood stolidly, uneasily tugging at his tangled beard.

"He's in a milder mood," murmured Gordon. "Easy, Hawkston. Let me handle this. I don't believe he'll have to be overpowered this time."

"In that case," said Hawkston, "I don't need you any longer."

Gordon whipped around; the Englishman's eyes were red with the killing lust, his hand rested on the butt of his pistol. For an instant the two men stood tensely facing one another. Hawkston spoke, almost in a whisper: "You fool, did you think I'd give you an even break? I don't need you to help me get Al Wazir back to el-Azem. I know a German doctor who can restore his mind if anybody can—and then I'll see that he tells me where to find the Blood of the Gods—"

Their right hands moved in a simultaneous blur of speed. Hawkston's gun cleared its holster as Gordon's scimitar flashed free. And the gun spoke just as the blade struck it, knocking it from the Englishman's hand. Gordon felt the wind of the slug and behind him the madman in the door grunted and fell heavily. The pistol rang on the stone and bounced from the ledge, and Gordon cut murderously at Hawkston's head, his eyes red with fury. A swift backward leap carried the Englishman out of range, and Hawkston tore out his scimitar as Gordon came at him in savage silence. The American had seen Al Wazir lying limp in the doorway, blood oozing from his head.

Gordon and Hawkston came together with a dazzling flame and crack of steel, in an unleashing of hard-pent passions, two wild natures a-thirst for each others' lives. Here was the urge to kill, loosed at last, and backing every blow.

For a few minutes stroke followed stroke too fast for the eye to distinguish, had any eye witnessed that onslaught. They fought with a chilled-steel fury, a reckless abandon that was yet neither wild or careless. The clang of steel was deafening; miraculously, it seemed, the shimmer of steel played about their heads, yet neither edge cut home. The skill of the two fighters was too well matched.

After the first hurricane of attack, the play changed subtly; it grew, not less savage but more crafty. The desert sun, that had lighted the blades of a thousand generations of swordsmen, in a land sworn to the sword, had never shone on a more scintillating display of swordsmanship than this, where two aliens carved out the destinies of their tangled careers on a high-flung ledge between sun and desert.

Up and down the ledge—scruff and shift of quick-moving feet—gliding, not stamping—ring and clash of steel meeting steel—flame-lighted black eyes glaring into flinty grey eyes; flying blades turned crimson by the rising sun.

Hawkston had cut his teeth on the straight blade of his native land, and he was partial to the point and used it with devilish skill. Gordon had learned sword fighting in the hard school of the Afghan mountain wars, with the curved tulwar, and he fought with no set or orthodox style. His blade was a lethal, living thing that darted like a serpent's tongue or lashed with devastating power.

Here was no ceremonious dueling with elegant rules and formalities. It was a fight for life, naked and desperate, and within the space of half a dozen minutes both men had attempted or foiled tricks that would have made a medieval Italian fencing master blink. There was no pause or breathing spell; only the constant slither and rasp of blade on blade—Hawkston failing in his attempt to maneuver Gordon about so the sun would dazzle his eyes; Gordon almost rushing Hawkston over the rim of the ledge, the Englishman saving himself by a sidewise leap.

The end came suddenly. Hawkston, with sweat pouring down his face, realized that the sheer strength in Gordon's arm was beginning to tell. Even his iron wrist was growing numb under the terrific blows the American rained on his guard. Believing himself to be superior to Gordon in pure fencing skill, he began the preliminaries of an intricate maneuver, and meeting with apparent success, feinted a cut at Gordon's head. El Borak knew it was a feint, but, pretending to be deceived by it, he lifted his sword as though to parry the cut. Instantly Hawkston's point licked at his throat. Even as the Englishman thrust he knew he had been tricked, but he could not check the motion. The blade passed over Gordon's shoulder as the American evaded the thrust with a swaying twist of his torso, and his scimitar flashed like white steel lightning in the sun. Hawkston's dark features were blotted out by a gush of blood and brains; his scimitar rang loud on the rocky ledge; he swayed, tottered, and fell suddenly, his crown split to the hinges of the jawbone.

Gordon shook the sweat from his eyes and glared down at the prostrate figure, too drunken with hate and battle to fully realize that his foe was dead. He started and whirled as a voice spoke weakly behind him: "The same swift blade as ever, El Borak!"

Al Wazir was sitting with his back against the wall. His eyes, no longer murky nor bloodshot, met Gordon's levelly. In spite of his tangled hair and beard there was something ineffably tranquil and seer-like about him. Here, indeed, was the man Gordon had known of old.

"Ivan! Alive! But Hawkston's bullet—"

"Was that what it was?" Al Wazir lifted a hand to his

head; it came away smeared with blood. "Anyway, I'm very much alive, and my mind's clear—for the first time in God knows how long. What happened?"

"You stopped a slug meant for me," grunted Gordon. "Let me see that wound." After a brief investigation he announced: "Just a graze; ploughed through the scalp and knocked you out. I'll wash it and bandage it." While he worked he said tersely: "Hawkston was on your trail; after your rubies. I tried to beat him here, and Shalan ibn Mansour trapped us both. You were a bit out of your head and I had to tie you up. We had a tussle with the Arabs and finally beat them off."

"What day is it?" asked Al Wazir. At Gordon's reply he ejaculated: "Great heavens! It's more than a month since I got knocked on the head!"

"What's that?" exclaimed Gordon. "I thought the loneliness—"

Al Wazir laughed. "Not that, El Borak. I was doing some excavation work—I discovered a shaft in one of the lower caves, leading down to the tunnel. The mouths of both were sealed with slabs of rock. I opened them up, just out of curiosity. Then I found another shaft leading from an upper cave to the summit of the cliff, like a chimney. It was while I was working out the slab that sealed it, that I dislodged a shower of rocks. One of them gave me an awful rap on the head. My mind's been a blank ever since, except for brief intervals—and they weren't very clear. I remember them like bits of dreams, now. I remember squatting in the Nest, tearing tins open and gobbling food, trying to remember who I was and why I was here. Then everything would fade out again.

"I have another vague recollection of being tied to a rock in the cave, and seeing you and Hawkston lying on the ledge, and firing. Of course I didn't know either of you. I remember hearing you saying that if somebody was killed the others would go away. There was a lot of shooting and shouting and that frightened me and hurt my ears. I wanted you all to go away and leave me in peace.

"I don't know how I got loose, but my next disjointed bit of memory is that of creeping up the shaft that leads to the top of the cliff, and then climbing, climbing, with the stars over me and the wind blowing in my face—heavens! I must have climbed over the summit of the hill and down the crags on the other side!

"Then I have a muddled remembrance of running and crawling through the dark—a confused impression of shooting and noise, and a man standing alone on a knoll and shouting—" he shuddered and shook his head. "When I try to remember what happened then, it's all a blind whirl of fire and blood, like a nightmare. Somehow I seemed to feel that the man on the knoll was to blame for all the noise that was maddening me, and that if he quit shouting, they'd all go away and let me alone. But from that point it's all a blind red mist."

Gordon held his peace. He realized that it was his remark, overheard by Al Wazir, that if Shalan ibn Mansour were slain, the Arabs would flee, which had taken root in the madman's clouded brain and provided the impulse—probably subconsciously—which finally translated itself into action. Al Wazir did not remember having killed the *shaykh*, and there was no use distressing him with the truth.

"I remember running, then," murmured Al Wazir, rubbing his head. "I was in a terrible fright, and trying to get back to the Caves. I remember climbing again—up, this time. I must have climbed back over the crags and down the chimney again—I'll wager I couldn't make that climb clothed in my right mind. The next thing I remember is hearing voices, and they sounded somehow familiar. I started toward them— then something cracked and flashed in my head, and I knew nothing more until I came to myself a few moments ago, in possession of all my faculties, and saw you and Hawkston fighting with your swords."

"You were evidently regaining your senses," said Gordon. "It took the extra jolt of that slug to set your numb machinery going again. Such things have happened before.

"Ivan, I've got a camel hidden nearby, and the Arabs left some ropes of hay in their camp when they pulled out. I'm going to feed and water it, and then—well, I intended taking you back to the Coast with me, but since you've regained your wits, I suppose you'll—"

"I'm going back with you," said Al Wazir. "My meditations didn't give me the gift of prophecy, but they convinced me—even before I got that rap on the head— that the best life a man can live is one of service to his fellow man. Just as you do, in your own way! I can't help mankind by dreaming out here in the desert." He glanced down at the prostrate figure on the ledge. "We'll have to build a cairn, first. Poor devil, it was his destiny to be the last sacrifice to the Blood of the Gods."

"What do you mean?"

"They were stained with men's blood," answered Al Wazir. "They have caused nothing but suffering and crime since they first appeared in history. Before I left el-Azem I threw them into the sea."

The Country of the Knife

CHAPTER I.

A Cry out of the East

A CRY FROM beyond the bolted door—a thick, desperate croaking that gaspingly repeated a name. Stuart Brent paused in the act of filling a whisky glass, and shot a startled glance toward the door from beyond which that cry had come. It was his name that had been gasped out—and why should anyone call on him with such frantic urgency at midnight in the hall outside his apartment?

He stepped to the door, without stopping to set down the square amber bottle. Even as he turned the knob, he was electrified by the unmistakable sounds of a struggle outside—the quick fierce scuff of feet, the thud of blows, then the desperate voice lifted again. He threw the door open.

The richly appointed hallway outside was dimly lighted by bulbs concealed in the jaws of gilt dragons writhing across the ceiling. The costly red rugs and velvet tapestries seemed to drink in this soft light, heightening an effect of unreality. But the struggle going on before his eyes was as real as life and death.

There were splashes of a brighter crimson on the dark-red rug. A man was down on his back before the door, a slender man whose white face shone like a wax mask in the dim light. Another man crouched upon him, one knee grinding brutally into his breast, one hand twisting at the victim's throat. The other hand lifted a red-smeared blade.

Brent acted entirely through impulse. Everything happened simultaneously. The knife was swinging up for the downward drive even as he opened the door. At the height of its arc it hovered briefly as the wielder shot a venomous, slit-eyed glance at the man in the doorway. In that instant Brent saw murder about to be done, saw that the victim was a white man, the killer a swarthy alien of some kind. Age-old implanted instincts acted through him, without his conscious volition. He dashed the heavy whisky bottle full into the dark face with all his power. The hard, stocky body toppled backward in a crash of broken glass and a shower of splattering liquor, and the knife rang on the floor several feet away. With a feline snarl the fellow bounced to his feet, red-eyed, blood and whisky streaming from his face and over his collar.

For an instant he crouched as if to leap at Brent barehanded. Then the glare in his eyes wavered, turned to something like fear, and he wheeled and was gone, lunging down the stair with reckless haste. Brent stared after him in amazement. The whole affair was fantastic, and Brent was irritated. He had broken a self-imposed rule of long standing—which was never to butt into anything which was not his business.

"Brent!" It was the wounded man, calling him weakly. Brent bent down to him.

"What is it, old fellow—Thunderation! Stockton!"

"Get me in, quick!" panted the other, staring fearfully at the stair. "He may come back—with others."

Brent stooped and lifted him bodily. Stockton was not a bulky man, and Brent's trim frame concealed the muscles of an athlete. There was no sound throughout the building. Evidently no one had been aroused by the muffled sounds of the brief fight. Brent carried the wounded man into the room and laid him carefully on a divan. There was blood on Brent's hands when he straightened.

"Lock the door!" gasped Stockton.

Brent obeyed, and then turned back, frowning concernedly down at the man. They offered a striking contrast—Stockton, light-haired, of medium height, frail, with plain, commonplace features now twisted in a grimace of pain, his sober garments disheveled and smeared with blood; Brent, tall, dark, immaculately tailored, handsome in a virile masculine way, and self-assured. But in Stockton's pale eyes there blazed a fire that burned away the difference between them, and gave the wounded man something that Brent did not possess—something that dominated the scene.

"You're hurt, Dick!" Brent caught up a fresh whisky bottle. "Why, man, you're stabbed to pieces! I'll call a doctor, and—"

"No!" A lean hand brushed aside the whisky glass and seized Brent's wrist. "It's no use. I'm bleeding inside. I'd be dead now, but I can't leave my job unfinished. Don't interrupt—just listen!"

Brent knew Stockton spoke the truth. Blood was oozing thinly from the wounds in his breast, where a thin-bladed knife must have struck home at least half a dozen times. Brent looked on, awed and appalled, as the small, bright-eyed man fought death to a standstill, gripping the last fading fringes of life and keeping himself conscious and lucid to the end by the sheer effort of an iron will.

"I stumbled on something big tonight, down in a water-front dive. I was looking for something else—uncovered this by accident. Then *they* got suspicious. I got away—came here because you were the only man I knew in San Francisco. But that devil was after me—caught me on the stair."

Blood oozed from the livid lips, and Stockton spat dryly. Brent looked on helplessly. He knew the man was a secret agent of the British government, who had made a business of tracing sinister secrets to their source. He was dying as he had lived, in the harness.

"Something big!" whispered the Englishman. "Something that balances the fate of India! I can't tell you all now—I'm going fast. But there's one man in the world who must know. You must find him, Brent! His name is Gordon—Francis Xavier Gordon. He's an American; the Afghans call him El Borak. I'd have gone to him—but you must go. Promise me!"

Brent did not hesitate. His soothing hand on the dying man's shoulder was even more convincing and reassuring than his quiet, level voice.

"I promise, old man. But where am I to find him?"

"Somewhere in Afghanistan. Go at once. Tell the police nothing. Spies are all around. If they know I knew you, and spoke with you before I died, they'll kill you before you can reach Gordon. Tell the police I was simply a drunken stranger, wounded by an unknown party, and staggering into your hall to die. You never saw me before. I said nothing before I died.

"Go to Kabul. The British officials will make your way easy that far. Simply say to each one: 'Remember the kites of Khoral Nulla.' That's your password. If Gordon isn't in Kabul, the ameer will give you an escort to hunt for him in the hills. You must find him! The peace of India depends on him, now!"

"But what shall I tell him?" Brent was bewildered.

"Say to him," gasped the dying man, fighting fiercely for a few more moments of life, "say: 'The Black Tigers had a new prince; they call him Abd el Khafid, but his real name is Vladimir Jakrovitch.'"

"Is that all?" This affair was growing more and more bizarre.

"Gordon will understand and act. The Black Tigers are your peril. They're a secret society of Asiatic murderers. Therefore, be on your guard at every step of the way. But El Borak will understand. He'll know where to look for Jakrovitch—in Rub el Harami—the Abode of Thieves—"

A convulsive shudder, and the slim threat that had held the life in the tortured body snapped.

Brent straightened and looked down at the dead man in wonder. He shook his head, marveling again at the inner unrest that sent men wandering in the waste places of the world, playing a game of life and death for a meager wage. Games that had gold for their stake Brent could understand—none better. His strong, sure fingers could read the cards almost as a man reads books; but he could not read the souls of men like Richard Stockton who stake their lives on the bare boards where Death is the dealer. What if the man won, how could he measure his winnings, where cash his chips? Brent asked no odds of life; he lost without a wince; but in winning, he was a usurer, demanding the last least crumb of the wager, and content with nothing less than the glittering, solid materialities of life. The grim and barren game Stockton had played held no promise for Stuart Brent, and to him the Englishman had always been a little mad.

But whatever Brent's faults or virtues, he had his code. He lived by it, and by it he meant to die. The foundation stone of that code was loyalty. Stockton had never saved Brent's life, renounced a girl both loved, exonerated him from a false accusation, or anything so dramatic. They had simply been boyhood friends in a certain British university, years ago, and years had passed between their occasional meetings since then. Stockton had no claim on Brent, except for their old friendship. But that was a tie as solid as a log chain, and the Englishman had known it, when, in the desperation of knowing himself doomed, he had crawled to Brent's door. And Brent had given his promise, and he intended making it good. It did not occur to him that there was any other alternative. Stuart Brent was the restless black sheep of an aristocratic old California family whose founder crossed the plains in an ox wagon in '49—and he had never welshed a bet nor let down a friend.

He turned his head and stared through a window, almost hidden by its satin curtains. He was comfortable here. His luck had been phenomenal of late. To-morrow evening there was a big poker game scheduled at his favorite club, with a fat Oklahoma oil king who was ripe for a cleaning. The races began at Tia Juana within a few days, and Brent had his eye on a slim sorrel gelding that ran like the flame of a prairie fire.

Outside, the fog curled and drifted, beading the pane. Pictures formed for him there—prophetic pictures of an East different from the colorful civilized East he had touched in his roamings. Pictures not at all like the European-dominated cities he remembered, exotic colors of veranda-shaded clubs, soft-footed servants laden with cooling drinks, languorous and beautiful women, white garments and sun helmets. Shiveringly he sensed a wilder, older East; it had blown a scent of itself to him out of the fog, over a knife stained with human blood. An East not soft and warm and exotic-colored, but bleak and grim and savage, where peace was not and law was a mockery, and life hung on the tilt of a balanced blade. The East known by Stockton, and this mysterious American they called "El Borak."

Brent's world was here, the world he had promised to abandon for a blind, quixotic mission; he knew nothing of that other leaner, fiercer world; but there was no hesitation in his manner as he turned toward the door.

CHAPTER II.

The Road to Rub El Harami

A WIND BLEW over the shoulders of the peaks where the snow lay drifted, a knife-edge wind that slashed through leather and wadded cloth in spite of the searing sun. Stuart Brent blinked his eyes against the glare of that intolerable sun, shivered at the bite of the wind. He had no coat, and his shirt was tattered. For the thousandth futile, involuntary time, he wrenched at the fetters on his wrists. They jangled, and the man riding in front of him cursed, turned and struck him heavily in the mouth. Brent reeled in his saddle, blood starting to his lips.

The saddle chafed him, and the stirrups were too short for his long legs. He was riding along a knife-edge trail, in the middle of a straggling line of some thirty men—ragged men on gaunt, ribby horses. They rode hunched in their high-peaked saddles, turbaned heads thrust forward and nodding in unison to the *clop-clop* of their horses' hoofs, long-barreled rifles swaying across the saddlebows. On one hand rose a towering cliff; on the other, a sheer precipice fell away into echoing depths. The skin was worn from Brent's wrists by the rusty, clumsy iron manacles that secured them; he was bruised from the kicks and blows, faint with hunger and giddy with the enormousness of the altitude. His nose bled at times without having been struck. Ahead of them loomed the backbone of the gigantic range that had risen like a rampart before them for so many days.

Dizzily he reviewed the events of the weeks that stretched between the time he had carried Dick Stockton, dying, into his flat, and this unbelievable, yet painfully real moment. The intervening period of time might have been an unfathomable and unbridgeable gulf stretching between and dividing two worlds that had nothing in common save consciousness.

He had come to India on the first ship he could catch. Official doors had opened to him at the whispered password: "Remember the kites of Khoral Nulla!" His path had been smoothed by impressive-looking documents with great red seals, by cryptic orders barked over telephones, or whispered into attentive ears. He had moved smoothly northward along hitherto unguessed channels. He had glimpsed, faintly, some of the shadowy, mountainous machinery grinding silently and ceaselessly behind the scenes—the unseen, half-suspected cogwheels of the empire that girdles the world.

Mustached men with medals on their breasts had conferred with him as to his needs, and quiet men in civilian clothes had guided him on his way. But no one had asked him why he sought El Borak, or what message he bore. The password and the mention of Stockton had sufficed. His friend had been more important in the imperial scheme of things than Brent had ever realized. The adventure had seemed more and more fantastic as he progressed—a page out of the "Arabian Nights," as he blindly carried a dead man's message, the significance of which he could not even guess, to a mysterious figure lost in the mists of the hills; while, at a whispered incantation, hidden doors swung wide and enigmatic figures bowed him on his way. But all this changed in the North.

Gordon was not in Kabul. This Brent learned from the

lips of no less than the ameer himself—wearing his European garments as if born to them, but with the sharp, restless eyes of a man who knows he is a pawn between powerful rivals, and whose nerves are worn thin by the constant struggle for survival. Brent sensed that Gordon was a staff on which the ameer leaned heavily. But neither king nor agents of empire could chain the American's roving foot, or direct the hawk flights of the man the Afghans called "El Borak," the "Swift."

And Gordon was gone—wandering alone into those naked hills whose bleak mysteries had long ago claimed him from his own kind. He might be gone a month, he might be gone a year. He might—and the ameer shifted uneasily at the possibility—never return. The crag-set villages were full of his blood enemies.

Not even the long arm of empire reached beyond Kabul. The ameer ruled the tribes after a fashion—with a dominance that dared not presume too far. This was the Country of the Hills, where law was hinged on the strong arm wielding the long knife.

Gordon had vanished into the Northwest. And Brent, though flinching at the grim nakedness of the Himalayas, did not hesitate or visualize an alternative. He asked for and received an escort of soldiers. With them he pushed on, trying to follow Gordon's trail through the mountain villages.

A week out of Kabul they lost all trace of him. To all effects Gordon had vanished into thin air. The wild, shaggy hillmen answered questions sullenly, or not at all, glaring at the nervous Kabuli soldiery from under black brows. The farther they got away from Kabul, the more open the hostility. Only once did a question evoke a spontaneous response, and that was a suggestion that Gordon had been murdered by hostile tribesmen. At that, sardonic laughter yelled up from the wild men—the fierce, mocking mirth of the hills. El Borak trapped by his enemies? Is the gray wolf devoured by the fat-tailed sheep? And another gust of dry, ironic laughter, as hard as the black crags that burned under a sun of liquid flame.

Stubborn as his grandsire who had glimpsed a mirage of tree-fringed ocean shore across the scorching desolation of another desert, Brent groped on, at a blind venture, trying to pick up the cold scent, far past the point of safety, as the gray-faced soldiers warned him again and again. They warned him that they were far from Kabul, in a sparsely settled, rebellious, little-explored region, whose wild people were rebels to the ameer, and enemies to El Borak. They would have deserted Brent long before and fled back to Kabul, had they not feared the ameer's wrath.

Their forebodings were justified in the hurricane of rifle fire that swept their camp in a chill gray dawn. Most of them fell at the first volley that ripped from the rocks about them. The rest fought futilely, ridden over and cut down by the wild riders that materialized out of the gray. Brent knew the surprise had been the soldiers' fault, but he did not have it in his heart to curse them, even now. They had been like children, sneaking in out of the cold as soon as his back was turned, sleeping on sentry duty, and lapsing into slovenly and unmilitary habits as soon as they were out of sight of Kabul. They had not wanted to come, in the first place; a foreboding of doom had haunted them; and now they were dead, and he was a captive, riding toward a fate he could not even guess.

Four days had passed since that slaughter, but he still turned sick when he remembered it—the smell of powder and blood, the screams, the rending chop of steel. He shuddered at the memory of the man he had killed in that last rush, with his pistol muzzle almost in the bearded face that lunged at him beneath a lifted rifle butt. He had never killed a man before. He sickened as he remembered the cries of the wounded soldiers when the conquerors cut their throats. And over and over he wondered why he had been spared—why they had overpowered and fettered him, instead of killing him. His suffering had been so intense he often wished they had killed him outright.

He was allowed to ride, and he was fed grudgingly when the others ate. But the food was niggardly. He who had never known hunger was never without it now, a gnawing misery. His coat had been taken from him, and the nights were a long agony in which he almost froze on the hard ground, in the icy winds. He wearied unto death of the day-long riding over incredible trails that wound up and up until he felt as if he could reach out a hand—if his hands were free—and touch the cold, pale sky. He was kicked and beaten until the first fiery resentment and humiliation had been dissolved in a dull hurt that was only aware of the physical pain, not of the injury to his self-respect.

He did not know who his captors were. They did not deign to speak English to him, but he had picked up more than a smattering of Pashto on that long journey up the Khyber to Kabul, and from Kabul westward. Like many men who live by their wits, he had the knack of acquiring new languages. But all he learned from listening to their conversation was that their leader was called Muhammad ez Zahir, and their destiny was Rub el Harami.

Rub el Harami! Brent had heard it first as a meaningless phrase gasped from Richard Stockton's blue lips. He had heard more of it as he came northward from the hot plains of the Punjab—a city of mystery and evil, which no white man had ever visited except as a captive, and from which none had ever escaped. A plague spot, sprawled in the high, bare hills, almost fabulous, beyond the reach of the ameer—an outlaw city, whence the winds blew whispered tales too fantastic and hideous for credence, even in this Country of the Knife.

At times Brent's escort mocked him, their burning eyes and grimly smiling lips lending a sinister meaning to their taunt: "The Feringi goes to Rub el Harami!"

For the pride of race he stiffened his spine and set his jaw; he plumbed unsuspected depths of endurance—legacy of a clean, athletic life, sharpened by the hard traveling of the past weeks.

They crossed a rocky crest and dropped down an incline between ridges that tilted up for a thousand feet.

Far above and beyond them they occasionally glimpsed a notch in the rampart that was the pass over which they must cross the backbone of the range up which they were toiling. It was as they labored up a long slope that the solitary horseman appeared.

The sun was poised on the knife-edge crest of a ridge to the west, a blood-colored ball, turning a streak of the sky to flame. Against that crimson ball a horseman appeared suddenly, a centaur image, black against the blinding curtain. Below him every rider turned in his saddle, and rifle bolts clicked. It did not need the barked command of Muhammed ez Zahir to halt the troop. There was something wild and arresting about that untamed figure in the sunset that held every eye. The rider's head was thrown back, the horse's long mane streaming in the wind.

Then the black silhouette detached itself from the crimson ball and moved down toward them, details springing into being as it emerged from the blinding background. It was a man on a rangy black stallion who came down the rocky, pathless slope with the smooth curving flight of an eagle, the sure hoofs spurning the ground. Brent, himself a horseman, felt his heart leap into his throat with admiration for the savage steed.

But he almost forgot the horse when the rider pulled up before them. He was neither tall nor bulky, but a barbaric strength was evident in his compact shoulders, his deep chest, his corded wrists. There was strength, too, in the keen, dark face, and the eyes, the blackest Brent had even seen, gleamed with an inward fire such as the American had seen burn in the eyes of wild things—an indomitable wildness and an unquenchable vitality. The thin, black mustache did not hide the hard set of the mouth.

The stranger looked like a desert dandy beside the ragged men of the troop, but it was a dandyism definitely masculine, from the silken turban to the silver-heeled boots. His bright-hued robe was belted with a gold-buckled girdle that supported a Turkish saber and a long dagger. A rifle jutted its butt from a scabbard beneath his knee.

• • •

Thirty-odd pairs of hostile eyes centered on him, after suspiciously sweeping the empty ridges behind him as he galloped up before the troop and reined his steed back on its haunches with a flourish that set the gold ornaments jingling on curb chains and reins. An empty hand was flung up in an exaggerated gesture of peace. The rider, well poised and confident, carried himself with a definite swagger.

"What do you want?" growled Muhammad ez Zahir, his cocked rifle covering the stranger.

"A small thing, as Allah is my witness!" declared the other, speaking Pashto with an accent Brent had never heard before. "I am Shirkuh, of Jebel Jawur. I ride to Rub el Harami. I wish to accompany you."

"Are you alone?" demanded Muhammad.

"I set forth from Herat many days ago with a party of camel men who swore they would guide me to Rub el Harami. Last night they sought to slay and rob me. One of them died suddenly. The others ran away, leaving me without food or guides. I lost my way, and have been wandering in the mountains all last night and all this day. Just now, by the favor of Allah, I sighted your band."

"How do you know we are bound for Rub el Harami?" demanded Muhammad.

"Are you not Muhammad ez Zahir, the prince of swordsmen?" countered Shirkuh.

The Afghan's beard bristled with satisfaction. He was not impervious to flattery. But he was still suspicious.

"You know me, Kurd?"

"Who does not know Muhammad ez Zahir? I saw you in the *suk* of Teheran, years ago. And now men say you are high in the ranks of the Black Tigers."

"Beware how your tongue runs, Kurd!" responded Muhammad. "Words are sometimes blades to cut men's throats. Are you sure of a welcome in Rub el Harami?"

"What stranger can be sure of a welcome there?" Shirkuh laughed. "But there is Feringi blood on my sword, and a price on my head. I have heard that such men were welcome in Rub el Harami."

"Ride with us if you will," said Muhammad. "I will get you through the Pass of Nadir Khan. But what may await you at the city gates is none of my affair. I have not invited you to Rub el Harami. I accept no responsibility for you."

"I ask for no man to vouch for me," retorted Shirkuh, with a glint of anger, brief and sharp, like the flash of hidden steel struck by a flint and momentarily revealed. He glanced curiously at Brent.

"Has there been a raid over the border?" he asked.

"This fool came seeking someone," scornfully answered Muhammad. "He walked into a trap set for him."

"What will be done with him in Rub el Harami?" pursued the newcomer, and Brent's interest in the conversation suddenly became painfully intense.

"He will be placed on the slave block," answered Muhammad, "according to the age-old custom of the city. Who bids highest will have him."

And so Brent learned the fate in store for him, and cold sweat broke out on his flesh as he contemplated a life spent as a tortured drudge to some turbaned ruffian. But he held up his head, feeling Shirkuh's fierce eyes upon him.

The stranger said slowly: "It may be his destiny to serve Shirkuh, of the Jebel Jawur! I never owned a slave—but who knows? It strikes my fancy to buy this Feringi!"

Brent reflected that Shirkuh must know that he was in no danger of being murdered and robbed, or he would never so openly imply possession of money. That suggested that he knew these were picked men, carrying out someone's instructions so implicitly that they could be depended on not to commit any crime not included in those orders. That implied organization and obedience beyond the conception of any ordinary hill chief. He was convinced that these men belonged to that mysterious cult against which Stockton had warned him—the Black Tigers. Then had their capture of him been due merely to chance? It seemed improbable.

"There are rich men in Rub el Harami, Kurd," growled Muhammad. "But it may be that none will want this Feringi and a wandering vagabond like you might buy him. Who knows?"

"Only in Allah is knowledge," agreed Shirkuh, and swung his horse into line behind Brent, crowding a man out of position and laughing when the Afghan snarled at him.

The troop got into motion, and a man leaned over to strike Brent with a rifle butt. Shirkuh checked the stroke. His lips laughed, but there was menace in his eyes.

"Nay! This infidel may belong to me before many days, and I will not have his bones broken!"

The man growled, but did not press the matter, and the troop rode on. They toiled up a ridge in a long shadow cast by the crag behind which the sun had sunk, and came into a valley and the sight of the sun again, just sinking behind a mountain. As they went down the slope, they spied white turbans moving among the crags to the west, and Muhammad ez Zahir snarled in suspicion at Shirkuh.

"Are they friends of yours, you dog? You said you were alone!"

"I know them not!" declared Shirkuh. Then he dragged his rifle from its boot. "The dogs fire on us!" For a tiny tongue of fire had jetted from among the boulders in the distance, and a bullet whined overhead.

"Hill-bred dogs who grudge us the use of the well ahead!" said Muhammad ez Zahir. "Would we had time to teach them a lesson! Hold your fire, you dogs! The range is too long for either they or us to do damage."

But Shirkuh wheeled out of the line of march and rode toward the foot of the ridge. Half a dozen men broke cover, high up on the slope, and dashed away over the crest, leaning low and spurring hard. Shirkuh fired once, then took steadier aim and fired three shots in swift succession.

"You missed!" shouted Muhammad angrily. "Who could hit at such a range?"

"Nay!" yelled Shirkuh. "Look!"

One of the ragged white shapes had wavered and pitched forward on its pony's neck. The beast vanished over the ridge, its rider lolling limply in the saddle.

"He will not ride far!" exulted Shirkuh, waving his rifle over his head as he raced back to the troop. "We Kurds have eyes like mountain hawks!"

"Shooting a Pathan hill thief does not make a hero," snapped Muhammad, turning disgustedly away.

But Shirkuh merely laughed tolerantly, as one so sure of his fame that he could afford to overlook the jealousies of lesser souls.

They rode on down into the broad valley, seeing no more of the hillmen. Dusk was falling when they halted beside the well. Brent, too stiff to dismount, was roughly jerked off his horse. His legs were bound, and he was allowed to sit with his back against a boulder just far enough away from the fires they built to keep him from benefiting any from the heat. No guard was set over him at present.

Presently Shirkuh came striding over to where the prisoner gnawed at the wretched crusts they allowed him. Shirkuh walked with a horseman's roll, setting his booted legs wide. He carried an iron bowl of stewed mutton, and some chupatties.

"Eat, Feringi!" he commanded roughly, but not harshly. "A slave whose ribs jut through his hide is no good to work or to fight. These niggardly Pathans would starve their grandfathers. But we Kurds are as generous as we are valiant!"

He offered the food with a gesture as of bestowing a province. Brent accepted it without thanks, and ate voraciously. Shirkuh had dominated the drama ever since he had entered it—a swashbuckler who swaggered upon the stage and would not be ignored. Even Muhammad ez Zahir was overshadowed by the overflowing vitality of the man. Shirkuh seemed a strange mixture of brutal barbarian and unsophisticated youth. There was a boyish exuberance in his swagger, and he displayed touches of naïve simplicity at times. But there was nothing childish about his glittering black eyes, and he moved with a tigerish suppleness that Brent knew could be translated instantly into a blur of murderous action.

Shirkuh thrust his thumbs in his girdle now and stood looking down at the American as he ate. The light from the nearest fire of dry tamarisk branches threw his dark face into shadowy half relief and gave it somehow an older, more austere look. The shadowy half light had erased the boyishness from his countenance, replacing it with a suggestion of somberness.

"Why did you come into the hills?" he demanded abruptly.

Brent did not immediately answer; he chewed on, toying with an idea. He was in as desperate a plight as he could be in, and he saw no way out. He looked about, seeing that his captors were out of earshot. He did not see the dim shape that squirmed up behind the boulder against which he leaned. He reached a sudden decision and spoke.

"Do you know the man called El Borak?"

Was there suspicion suddenly in the black eyes?

"I have heard of him," Shirkuh replied warily.

"I came into the hills looking for him. Can you find him? If you could get a message to him, I would pay you thirty thousand rupees."

Shirkuh scowled, as if torn between suspicion and avarice.

"I am a stranger in these hills," he said. "How could I find El Borak?"

"Then help me to escape," urged Brent. "I will pay you an equal sum."

Shirkuh tugged his mustache.

"I am one sword against thirty," he growled. "How do I know I would be paid? Feringi are all liars. I am an outlaw with a price on my head. The Turks would flay me, the Russians would shoot me, the British would hang me. There is nowhere I can go except to Rub el Harami. If I helped you to escape, that door would be barred against me, too."

"I will speak to the British for you," urged Brent. "El

Borak has power. He will secure a pardon for you."

He believed what he said; besides, he was in that desperate state when a man is likely to promise anything.

Indecision flickered in the black eyes, and Shirkuh started to speak, then changed his mind, turned on his heel, and strode away. A moment later the spy crouching behind the boulders glided away without having been discovered by Brent, who sat staring in despair after Shirkuh.

Shirkuh went straight to Muhammad, gnawing strips of dried mutton as he sat cross-legged on a dingy sheepskin near a small fire on the other side of the well. Shirkuh got there before the spy did.

"The Feringi has offered me money to take a word to El Borak," he said abruptly. "Also to aid him to escape. I bade him go to Jehannum, of course. In the Jebel Jawur I have heard of El Borak, but I have never seen him. Who is he?"

"A devil," growled Muhammad ez Zahir. "An American, like this dog. The tribes about the Khyber are his friends, and he is an adviser of the ameer, and an ally of the rajah, though he was once an outlaw. He has never dared come to Rub el Harami. I saw him once, three years ago, in the fight by Kalat-i-Ghilzai, where he and his cursed Afridis broke the back of the revolt that had else unseated the ameer. If we could catch him, Abd el Khafid would fill our mouths with gold."

"Perhaps this Feringi knows where to find him!" exclaimed Shirkuh, his eyes burning with a glitter that might have been avarice. "I will go to him and swear to deliver his message, and so trick him into telling me what he knows of El Borak."

"It is all one to me," answered Muhammad indifferently. "If I had wished to know why he came into the hills, I would have tortured it out of him before now. But my orders were merely to capture him and bring him alive to Rub el Harami. I could not turn aside, not even to capture El Borak. But if you are admitted into the city, perhaps

Abd el Khafid will give you a troop to go hunting El Borak."

"I will try!"

"Allah grant you luck," said Muhammad. "El Borak is a dog. I would myself give a thousand rupees to see him hanging in the market place."

"If it be the will of Allah, you shall meet El Borak!" said Shirkuh, turning away.

Doubtless it was the play of the firelight on his face which caused his eyes to burn as they did, but Muhammad felt a curious chill play down his spine, though he could not reason why.

Shirkuh's booted feet crunched away through the shale, and a furtive, ragged shadow came out of the night and squatted at Muhammad's elbow.

"I spied on the Kurd and the infidel as you ordered," muttered the spy. "The Feringi offered Shirkuh thirty thousand rupees either to seek out El Borak and deliver a message to him, or to aid him to escape us. Shirkuh lusted for the gold, but he has been outlawed by all the Feringis, and he dares not close the one door open to him."

"Good," growled Muhammad in his beard. "Kurds are dogs; it is well that this one is in no position to bite. I will speak for him at the pass. He does not guess the choice that awaits him at the gates of Rub el Harami."

Brent was sunk in the dreamless slumber of exhaustion, despite the hardness of the rocky ground and the chill of the night. An urgent hand shook him awake, an urgent whisper checked his startled exclamation. He saw a vague shape bending over him, and heard the snoring of his guard a few feet away. Guarding a man bound and fettered was more or less of a formality of routine. Shirkuh's voice hissed in Brent's ear.

"Tell me the message you wished to send El Borak! Be swift, before the guard awakes. I could not take the message when we talked before, for there was a cursed spy listening behind that rock. I told Muhammad what passed between us, because I knew the spy would tell him anyway, and I wished to disarm suspicion before it took root. Tell me the word!"

Brent accepted the desperate gamble.

"Tell him that Richard Stockton died, but before he died, he said this: 'The Black Tigers have a new prince; they call him Abd el Khafid, but his real name is Vladimir Jakrovitch.' This man dwells in Rub el Harami, Stockton told me."

"I understand," muttered Shirkuh. "El Borak shall know."

"But what of me?" urged Brent.

"I cannot help you escape now," muttered Shirkuh. "There are too many of them. All the guards are not asleep. Armed men patrol the outskirts of the camp, and others watch the horses—my own among them."

"I cannot pay you unless I get away!" argued Brent.

"That is in the lap of Allah!" hissed Shirkuh. "I must slip back to my blankets now, before I am missed. Here is a cloak against the chill of the night."

Brent felt himself enveloped in a grateful warmth, and then Shirkuh was gone, gliding away in the night with boots that made no more noise than the moccasins of a red Indian. Brent lay wondering if he had done the right thing. There was no reason why he should trust Shirkuh. But if he had done no good, at least he could not see that he had done any harm, either to himself, El Borak, or those interests menaced by the mysterious Black Tigers. He was a drowning man, clutching at straws. At last he went to sleep again, lulled by the delicious warmth of the cloak Shirkuh had thrown over him, and hoping that he would slip away in the night and ride to find Gordon— wherever he might be wandering.

CHAPTER III.

Shirkuh's Jest.

IT WAS SHIRKUH, however, who brought the American's breakfast to him the next morning. Shirkuh made no sign either of friendship or enmity, beyond a gruff admonition to eat heartily, as he did not wish to buy a skinny slave. But that might have been for the benefit of the guard yawning and stretching near by. Brent reflected that the cloak was sure evidence that Shirkuh had visited him in the night, but no one appeared to notice it.

As he ate, grateful at least for the good food, Brent was torn between doubts and hopes. He swung between half-hearted trust and complete mistrust of the man. Kurds were bred in deception and cut their teeth on treachery. Why should that offer of help not have been a trick to curry favor with Muhammad ez Zahir? Yet Brent realized that if Muhammad had wished to learn the reason for his presence in the hills, the Afghan would have been more likely to resort to torture than an elaborate deception. Then Shirkuh, like all Kurds, must be avaricious, and that was Brent's best chance. And if Shirkuh delivered the message, he must go further and help Brent to escape, in order to get his reward, for Brent, a slave in Rub el Harami, could not pay him thirty thousand rupees. One service necessitated the other, if Shirkuh hoped to profit by the deal. Then there was El Borak; if he got the message, he would learn of Brent's plight, and he would hardly fail to aid a fellow Feringi in adversity. It all depended now on Shirkuh.

Brent stared intently at the supple rider, etched against the sharp dawn. There was nothing of the Turanian or the Semite in Shirkuh's features. In the Iranian highlands there must be many clans who kept their ancient Aryan lineage pure. Shirkuh, in European garments, and without that Oriental mustache, would pass unnoticed in any Western crowd, but for that primordial blaze in his restless black eyes. They reflected an untamable soul. How could he expect this barbarian to deal with him according to the standards of the Western world?

They were pressing on before sunup, and their trail always led up now, higher and higher, through knife cuts in solid masses of towering sandstone, and along narrow paths that wound up and up interminably, until Brent was gasping again with the rarefied air of the high places. At high noon, when the wind was knife-edged with ice, and the sun was a splash of molten fire, they reached the Pass of Nadir Khan—a narrow cut winding tortuously for a mile between turrets of dull colored rock. A squat mud-and-stone tower stood in the mouth, occupied by ragged warriors squatting on their aerie like vultures. The troop halted until Muhammad ez Zahir was recognized. He vouched for the cavalcade, Shirkuh included, with a wave of his hand, and the rifles on the tower were lowered. Muhammad rode on into the pass, the others filing after him. Brent felt despairingly as if one prison door had already slammed behind him.

They halted for the midday meal in the corridor of the pass, shaded from the sun and sheltered from the wind. Again Shirkuh brought food to Brent, without comment or objection from the Afghans. But when Brent tried to catch his eye, he avoided the American's gaze.

After they left the pass, the road pitched down in long curving sweeps, through successively lower mountains that ran away and away like gigantic stairsteps from the crest of the range. The trail grew plainer, more traveled, but night found them still among the hills.

When Shirkuh brought food to Brent that night as usual, the American tried to engage him in conversation, under cover of casual talk for the benefit of the Afghan detailed to guard the American that night, who lolled near by, bolting chupatties.

"Is Rub el Harami a large city?" Brent asked.

"I have never been there," returned Shirkuh, rather shortly.

"Is Abd el Khafid the ruler?" persisted Brent.

"He is emir of Rub el Harami," said Shirkuh.

"And prince of the Black Tigers," spoke up the Afghan guard unexpectedly. He was in a garrulous mood, and he saw no reason for secrecy. One of his hearers would soon be a slave in Rub el Harami, the other, if accepted, a member of the clan.

"I am myself a Black Tiger," the guard boasted. "All in this troop are Black Tigers, and picked men. We are the lords of Rub el Harami."

"Then all in the city are not Black Tigers?" asked Brent.

"All are thieves. Only thieves live in Rub el Harami. But not all are Black Tigers. But it is the headquarters of the clan, and the prince of the Black Tigers is always emir of Rub el Harami."

"Who ordered my capture?" inquired Brent. "Muhammad ez Zahir?"

"Muhammad only does as he is ordered," returned the guard. "None gives orders in Rub el Harami save Abd el Khafid. He is absolute lord save where the customs of the city are involved. Not even the prince of the Black Tigers can change the customs of Rub el Harami. It was a city of thieves before the days of Genghis Khan. What its name was first, none knows; the Arabs call it Rub el Harami, the Abode of Thieves, and the name has stuck."

"It is an outlaw city?"

"It has never owned a lord save the prince of the Black Tigers," boasted the guard. "It pays no taxes to any save him—and to Shaitan."

"What do you mean, to Shaitan?" demanded Shirkuh.

"It is an ancient custom," answered the guard. "Each year a hundredweight of gold is given as an offering to Shaitan, so the city shall prosper. It is sealed in a secret cave somewhere near the city, but where no man knows, save the prince and the council of imams."

"Devil worship!" snorted Shirkuh. "It is an offense to Allah!"

"It is an ancient custom," defended the guard.

Shirkuh strode off, as if scandalized, and Brent lapsed into disappointed silence. He wrapped himself in Shirkuh's cloak as well as he could and slept.

They were up before dawn and pushing through the hills until they breasted a sweeping wall, down which the trail wound, and saw a rocky plain set in the midst of bare mountain chains, and the flat-topped towers of Rub el Harami rising before them.

They had not halted for the midday meal. As they neared the city, the trail became a well-traveled road. They overtook or met men on horses, men walking and driving laden mules. Brent remembered that it had been said that only stolen goods entered Rub el Harami. Its inhabitants were the scum of the hills, and the men they encountered looked it. Brent found himself comparing them with Shirkuh. The man was a wild outlaw, who boasted of his bloody crimes, but he was a clean-cut barbarian. He differed from these as a gray wolf differs from mangy alley curs.

He eyed all they met or passed with a gaze half naïve, half challenging. He was boyishly interested; he was ready to fight at the flick of a turban end, and gave the road to no man. He was the youth of the world incarnated, credulous, merry, hot-headed, generous, cruel, and arrogant. And Brent knew his life hung on the young savage's changing whims.

• • •

Rub el Harami was a walled city standing in the narrow rock-strewn plain hemmed in by bare hills. A battery of field pieces could have knocked down its walls with a dozen volleys—but the army never marched that could have dragged field pieces over the road that led to it through the Pass of Nadir Khan. Its gray walls loomed bleakly above the gray dusty waste of the small plain. A chill wind from the northern peaks brought a tang of snow and started the dust spinning. Well curbs rose gauntly here and there on the plain, and near each well stood a cluster of squalid huts. Peasants in rags bent their backs over sterile patches that yielded grudging crops—mere smudges on the dusty expanse. The low-hanging sun turned the dust to a bloody haze in the air, as the troop with its prisoner trudged on weary horses across the plain to the gaunt city.

Beneath a lowering arch, flanked by squat watchtowers, an iron-bolted gate stood open, guarded by a dozen swashbucklers whose girdles bristled with daggers. They clicked the bolts of their German rifles and stared arrogantly about them, as if itching to practice on some living target.

The troop halted, and the captain of the guard swaggered forth, a giant with bulging muscles and a henna-stained beard.

"Thy names and business!" he roared, glaring intolerantly at Brent.

"My name you know as well as you know your own," growled Muhammad ez Zahir. "I am taking a prisoner into the city, by order of Abd el Khafid."

"Pass, Muhammad ez Zahir," growled the captain. "But who is this Kurd?"

Muhammad grinned wolfishly, as if at a secret jest.

"An adventurer who seeks admission—Shirkuh, of the Jebel Jawur."

While they were speaking, a richly clad, powerfully built man on a white mare rode out of the gate and halted, unnoticed, behind the guardsmen. The henna-bearded captain turned toward Shirkuh who had dismounted to get a pebble out of his stallion's hoof.

"Are you one of the clan?" he demanded. "Do you know the secret signs?"

"I have not yet been accepted," answered Shirkuh, turning to face him. "Men tell me I must be passed upon by the council of imams."

"Aye, if you reach them! Does any chief of the city speak for you?"

"I am a stranger," replied Shirkuh shortly.

"We like not strangers in Rub el Harami," said the captain. "There are but three ways a stranger may enter the city. As a captive, like that infidel dog yonder; as one vouched for and indorsed by some established chief of the city; or"—he showed yellow fangs in an evil grin—"as the slayer of some fighting man of the city!"

He shifted the rifle to his right hand and slapped the butt with his left palm. Sardonic laughter rose about them, the dry, strident, cruel cackling of the hills. Those who laughed knew that in any kind of fight between a stranger and a man of the city every foul advantage would be taken. For a stranger to be forced into a formal duel with a Black Tiger was tantamount to signing his death warrant. Brent, rigid with sudden concern, guessed this from the vicious laughter.

But Shirkuh did not seem abashed.

"It is an ancient custom?" he asked naïvely, dropping a hand to his girdle.

"Ancient as Islam!" assured the giant captain, towering above him. "A tried warrior, with weapons in his hands, thou must slay!"

"Why, then—"

Shirkuh laughed, and as he laughed, he struck. His motion was as quick as the blurring stroke of a cobra. In one movement he whipped the dagger from his girdle and struck upward under the captain's bearded chin. The Afghan had no opportunity to defend himself, no chance to lift rifle or draw sword. Before he realized Shirkuh's intention, he was down, his life gushing out of his sliced jugular.

An instant of stunned silence was broken by wild yells of laughter from the lookers-on and the men of the troop. It was just such a devilish jest as the bloodthirsty hill natures appreciated. There is humor in the hills, but it is a fiendish humor. The strange youth had shown a glint of the hard wolfish sophistication that underlay his apparent callowness.

But the other guardsmen cried out angrily and surged forward, with a sharp rattle of rifle bolts. Shirkuh sprang back and tore his rifle from its saddle scabbard. Muhammad and his men looked on cynically. It was none of their affair. They had enjoyed Shirkuh's grim and bitter jest; they would equally enjoy the sight of him being shot down by his victim's comrades.

But before a finger could crook on a trigger, the man on the white mare rode forward, beating down the rifles of the guards with a riding whip.

"Stop!" he commanded. "The Kurd is in the right. He slew according to the law. The man's weapons were in his hands, and he was a tried warrior."

"But he was taken unaware!" they clamored.

"The more fool he!" was the callous retort. "The law makes no point of that. I speak for the Kurd. And I am Alafdal Khan, once of Waziristan."

"Nay, we know you, my lord!" The guardsmen salaamed profoundly.

Muhammad ez Zahir gathered up his reins and spoke to Shirkuh.

"You luck still holds, Kurd!"

"Allah loves brave men!" Shirkuh laughed, swinging into the saddle.

Muhammad ez Zahir rode under the arch, and the troop streamed after him, their captive in their midst. They traversed a short narrow street, winding between walls of mud and wood, where overhanging balconies almost touched each other over the crooked way. Brent saw women staring at them through the lattices. The cavalcade emerged into a square much like that of any other hill town. Open shops and stalls lined it, and it was thronged by a colorful crowd. But there was a difference. The crowd was too heterogeneous, for one thing; then there was too much wealth in sight. The town was prosperous, but with a sinister, unnatural prosperity. Gold and silk gleamed on barefooted ruffians whose proper garb was rags, and the goods displayed in the shops seemed mute evidence of murder and pillage. This was in truth a city of thieves.

The throng was lawless and turbulent, its temper set on a hair trigger. There were human skulls nailed above the gate, and in an iron cage made fast to the wall Brent saw a human skeleton. Vultures perched on the bars. Brent felt cold sweat bead his flesh. That might well be his own fate—to starve slowly in an iron cage hung above the heads of the jeering crowd. A sick abhorrence and a fierce hatred of this vile city swept over him.

As they rode into the city, Alafdal Khan drew his mare alongside Shirkuh's stallion. The Waziri was a bull-shouldered man with a bushy purple-stained beard and wide, ox-like eyes.

"I like you, Kurd," he announced. "You are in truth a mountain lion. Take service with me. A masterless man is a broken blade in Rub el Harami."

"I thought Abd el Khafid was master of Rub el Harami," said Shirkuh.

"Aye! But the city is divided into factions, and each man who is wise follows one chief or the other. Only picked men with long years of service behind them are chosen for Abd el Khafid's house troops. The others follow various lords, who are each responsible to the emir."

"I am my own man!" boasted Shirkuh. "But you spoke for me at the gate. What devil's custom is this, when a stranger must kill a man to enter?"

"In old times it was meant to test a stranger's valor, and

make sure that each man who came into Rub el Harami was a tried warrior," said Alafdal. "For generations, however, it has become merely an excuse to murder strangers. Few come uninvited. You should have secured the patronage of some chief of the clan before you came. Then you could have entered the city peacefully."

"I knew no man in the clan," muttered Shirkuh. "There are no Black Tigers in the Jebel Jawur. But men say the clan is coming to life, after slumbering in idleness for a hundred years, and—"

A disturbance in the crowd ahead of them interrupted him. The people in the square had massed thickly about the troop, slowing their progress, and growling ominously at the sight of Brent. Curses were howled, and bits of offal and refuse thrown, and now a scarred Shinwari stooped and caught up a stone which he cast at the white man. The missile grazed Brent's ear, drawing blood, and with a curse Shirkuh drove his horse against the fellow, knocking him down. A deep roar rose from the mob, and it surged forward menacingly. Shirkuh dragged his rifle from under his knee, but Alafdal Khan caught his arm

"Nay, brother! Do not fire. Leave these dogs to me."

He lifted his voice in a bull's bellow which carried across the square.

"Peace, my children! This is Shirkuh, of Jebel Jawur, who has come to be one of us. I speak for him—I, Alafdal Khan!"

A cheer rose from the crowd whose spirit was as vagrant and changeable as a leaf tossed in the wind. Obviously the Waziri was popular in Rub el Harami, and Brent guessed why as he saw Alafdal thrust a hand into a money pouch he carried at his girdle. But before the chief could completely mollify the mob by flinging a handful of coins among them, another figure entered the central drama. It was a Ghilzai who reined his horse through the crowd—a slim man, but tall and broad-shouldered, and one who looked as though his frame were of woven steel wires. He wore a rose-colored turban; a rich girdle clasped his supple waist, and his caftan was embroidered with gilt thread. A clump of ruffians on horseback followed him.

He drew rein in front of Alafdal Khan, whose beard instantly bristled while his wide eyes dilated truculently. Shirkuh quietly exchanged his rifle for his saber.

"That is my man your Kurd rode down," said the Ghilzai, indicating the groaning ruffian now dragging his bleeding hulk away. "Do you set your men on mine in the streets, Alafdal Khan?"

The people fell tensely silent, their own passions forgotten in the rivalry of the chiefs. Even Brent could tell that this was no new antagonism, but the rankling of an old quarrel. The Ghilzai was alert, sneering, coldly provocative. Alafdal Khan was belligerent, angry, yet uneasy.

"Your man began it, Ali Shah," he growled. "Stand aside. We take a prisoner to the Adobe of the Damned."

Brent sensed that Alafdal Khan was avoiding the issue. Yet he did not lack followers. Hard-eyed men with weapons in their girdles, some on foot, some on horseback, pushed through the throng and ranged themselves behind the Waziri. It was not physical courage Alafdal lacked, but some fiber of decision.

At Alafdal's declaration, which placed him in the position of one engaged in the emir's business, and therefore not to be interfered with—a statement at which Muhammad ez Zahir smiled cynically—Ali Shah hesitated, and the tense instant might have smoldered out, had it not been for one of the Ghilzai's men—a lean Orakzai, with hashish madness in his eyes. Standing in the edge of the crowd, he rested a rifle over the shoulder of the man in front of him and fired point-blank at the Waziri chief. Only the convulsive start of the owner of the shoulder saved Alafdal Khan. The bullet tore a piece out of his turban, and before the Orakzai could fire again, Shirkuh rode at him and cut him down with a stroke that split his head to the teeth.

It was like throwing a lighted match into a powder mill. In an instant the square was a seething battle ground,

where the adherents of the rival chiefs leaped at each
others' throats with all the zeal ordinary men generally
display in fighting somebody else's battle. Muhammad ez
Zahir, unable to force his way through the heaving mass,
stolidly drew his troopers in a solid ring around his
prisoner. He had not interfered when the stones were cast.
Stones would not kill the Feringi, and he was concerned
only in getting Brent to his master alive and able to talk.
He did not care how bloody and battered he might be. But
in this mêlée a chance stroke might kill the infidel. His
men faced outward, beating off attempts to get at their
prisoner. Otherwise they took no part in the fighting. This
brawl between rival chiefs, common enough in Rub el
Harami, was none of Muhammad's affair.

Brent watched fascinated. But for modern weapons it
might have been a riot in ancient Babylon, Cairo, or
Nineveh—the same old jealousies, same old passions,
same old instinct of the common man fiercely to take up
some lordling's quarrel. He saw gaudily clad horsemen
curvetting and caracoling as they slashed at each other
with tulwars that were arcs of fire in the setting sun, and
he saw ragged rascals belaboring each other with staves
and cobblestones. No more shots were fired; it seemed an
unwritten law that firearms were not to be used in street
fighting. Or perhaps ammunition was too precious for
them to waste on each other.

But it was bloody enough while it lasted, and it littered
the square with stunned and bleeding figures. Men with
broken heads went down under the stamping hoofs, and
some of them did not get up again. Ali Shah's retainers
outnumbered Alafdal Khan's, but the majority of the
crowd were for the Waziri, as evidenced by the fragments
of stone and wood that whizzed about the ears of his
enemies. One of these well-meant missiles almost proved
their champion's undoing. It was a potsherd, hurled with
more zeal than accuracy at Ali Shah. It missed him and
crashed full against Alafdal's bearded chin with an impact
that filled the Waziri's eyes with tears and stars.

As he reeled in his saddle, his sword arm sinking, Ali

Shah spurred at him, lifting his tulwar. There was murder in the air, while the blinded giant groped dazedly, sensing his peril. But Shirkuh was between them, lunging through the crowd like a driven bolt. He caught the swinging tulwar on his saber, and struck back, rising in his stirrups to add force to the blow. His blade struck flat, but it broke the left arm Ali Shah threw up in desperation, and beat down on the Ghilzai's turban with a fury that stretched the chief bleeding and senseless on the trampled cobblestones.

A gratified yell went up from the crowd, and Ali Shah's men fell back, confused and intimidated. Then there rose a thunder of hoofs, and a troop of men in compact formation swept the crowd to right and left as they plunged ruthlessly through. They were tall men in black chain armor and spired helmets, and their leader was a black-bearded Yusufzai, resplendent in gold-chased steel.

"Give way!" he ordered, with the hard arrogance of authority. "Clear the *suk*, in the name of Abd el Khafid, emir of Rub el Harami!"

"The Black Tigers!" muttered the people, giving back, but watching Alafdal Khan expectantly.

For an instant it seemed that the Waziri would defy the riders. His beard bristled, his eyes dilated—then he wavered, shrugged his giant shoulders, and sheathed his tulwar.

"Obey the law, my children," he advised them, and, not to be cheated out of the gesture he loved, he reached into his bulging pouch and sent a golden shower over their heads.

They went scrambling after the coins, shouting, and cheering, and laughing, and somebody yelled audaciously:

"Hail, Alafdal Khan, emir of Rub el Harami!"

Alafdal's countenance was an almost comical mingling of vanity and apprehension. He eyed the Yusufzai captain sidewise half triumphantly, half uneasily, tugging at his purple beard. The captain said crisply:

"Let there be an end to this nonsense. Alafdal Khan, the emir will hold you to account if any more fighting occurs. He is weary of this quarrel."

"Ali Shah started it!" roared the Waziri heatedly.

The crowd rumbled menacingly behind him, stooping furtively for stones and sticks. Again that half-exultant, half-frightened look flitted across Alafdal's broad face. The Yusufzai laughed sardonically.

"Too much popularity in the streets may cost a man his head in the palace!" said he, and turning away, he began clearing the square.

The mob fell back sullenly, growling in their beards, not exactly flinching from the prodding lances of the riders, but retiring grudgingly and with menace in their bearing. Brent believed that all they needed to rise in bloody revolt was a determined leader. Ali Shah's men picked up their senseless chief and lifted him into his saddle; they moved off across the *suk* with the leader lolling drunkenly in their midst. The fallen men who were able to stand were hustled to their feet by the Black Tigers.

Alafdal glared after them in a curiously helpless anger, his hand in his purple beard. Then he rumbled like a bear and rode off with his men, the wounded ones swaying on the saddles of their companions. Shirkuh rode with him, and as he reined away, he shot a glance at Brent which the American hoped meant that he was not deserting him.

Muhammad ez Zahir led his men and captive out of the square and down a winding street, cackling sardonically in his beard as he went.

"Alafdal Khan is ambitious and fearful, which is a sorry combination. He hates Ali Shah, yet avoids bringing the feud to a climax. He would like to be emir of Rub el Harami, but he doubts his own strength. He will never do anything but guzzle wine and throw money to the multitude. The fool! Yet he fights like a hungry bear once he is roused."

A trooper nudged Brent and pointed ahead of them to a squat building with iron-barred windows.

"The Abode of the Damned, Feringi!" he said

maliciously. "No prisoner ever escaped therefrom—and none ever spent more than one night there."

At the door Muhammad give his captive in charge of a one-eyed Sudozai with a squad of brutal-looking blacks armed with whips and bludgeons. These led him up a dimly lighted corridor to a cell with a barred door. Into this they thrust him. They placed on the floor a vessel of scummy water and a flat loaf of moldy bread, and then filed out. The key turned in the lock with a chillingly final sound.

A few last rays of the sunset's afterglow found their way through the tiny, high, thick-barred window. Brent ate and drank mechanically, a prey to sick forebodings. All his future hinged now on Shirkuh, and Brent felt it was a chance as thin as a sword edge. Stiffly he stretched himself on the musty straw heaped in one corner. As he sank to sleep, he wondered dimly if there had ever really been a trim, exquisitely tailored person named Stuart Brent who slept in a soft bed and drank iced drinks out of slim-stemmed glasses, and danced with pink-and-white visions of feminine loveliness under tinted electric lights. It was a far-off dream; this was reality—rotten straw that crawled with vermin, smelly water and stale bread, and the scent of spilled blood that still seemed to cling to his garments after the fight in the square.

CHAPTER IV.

Crooked Paths.

BRENT AWOKE WITH the light of a torch dazzling his eyes. This torch was placed in a socket in the wall, and when his eyes became accustomed to the wavering glare, he saw a tall, powerful man in a long satin caftan and a green turban with a gold brooch. From beneath this turban, wide gray eyes, as cold as a sword of ice, regarded him contemplatively.

"You are Stuart Brent."

It was a statement, not a question. The man spoke English with only a hint of an accent; but that hint was unmistakable. Brent made no reply. This was Abd el Khafid, of course, but it was like meeting a character of fable clothed in flesh. Abd el Khafid and El Borak had begun to take on the appearance in Brent's worn brain of symbolic will-o'-the-wisps, nonexistent twin phantoms luring him to his doom. But here stood half of that phantasm, living and speaking. Perhaps El Borak was equally real, after all.

Brent studied the man almost impersonally. He looked Oriental enough in that garb, with his black pointed beard. But his hands were too big for a high-caste Moslem's hands—sinewy, ruthless hands that looked as if they could grasp either a sword hilt or a scepter. The body under the caftan appeared hard and capable—not with the tigerish suppleness of Shirkuh, but strong and quick, nevertheless.

"My spies watched you all the way from San Francisco," said Abd el Khafid. "They knew when you bought a steamship ticket to India. Their reports were wired by relays to Kabul—I have my secret wireless sets and spies in every capital of Asia—and thence here. I have my wireless set hidden back in the hills, here. Inconvenient, but the people would not stand for it in the city. It was a violation of custom. Rub el Harami rests on a foundation of customs—irksome at times, but mostly useful.

"I knew you would not have immediately sailed for India had not Richard Stockton told you something before he died, and I thought at first of having you killed as soon as you stepped off the ship. Then I decided to wait a bit and try to learn just how much you knew before I had you removed. Spies sent me word that you were coming North—that apparently you had told the British only that you wished to find El Borak. I knew then that Stockton had told you to find El Borak and tell him my true identity. Stockton was a human bloodhound, but it was only through the indiscretion of a servant that he learned the secret.

"Stockton knew that the only man who could harm me was El Borak. I am safe from the English here, safe from the ameer. El Borak could cause me trouble, if he suspected my true identity. As it is, so long as he considers me merely Abd el Khafid, a Moslem fanatic from Samarkand, he will not interfere. But if he should learn who I really am, he would guess why I am here, and what I am doing.

"So I let you come up the Khyber unmolested. It was evident by this time that you intended giving the news directly to El Borak, and my spies told me El Borak had vanished in the hills. I knew when you left Kabul, searching for him, and I sent Muhammad ez Zahir to capture and bring you here. You were easy to trace—a *Melakani* wandering in the hills with a band of Kabuli soldiery. So you entered Rub el Harami at last the only way an infidel may enter—as a captive, destined for the slave block."

"You are an infidel," retorted Brent. "If I expose your true identity to these people—"

The strong shoulders under the caftan shrugged.

"The imams know I was born a Russian. They know likewise that I am a true Moslem—that I foreswore Christianity and publicly acknowledged Islam, years ago. I cut all ties that bound me to *Feringistan*. My name is Abd el Khafid. I have a right to wear this green turban. I am a hadji. I have made the pilgrimage to Mecca. Tell the people of Rub el Harami that I am a Christian. They will laugh at you. To the masses I am a Moslem like themselves; to the council of imams I am a true convert."

Brent said nothing; he was in a trap he could not break.

"You are but a fly in my web," said Abd el Khafid contemptuously. "So unimportant that I intend to tell you my full purpose. It is good practice speaking in English. Sometimes I almost forget European tongues.

"The Black Tigers compose a very ancient society. It originally grew out of the bodyguard of Genghis Khan. After his death they settled in Rub el Harami, even then an outlaw city, and became the ruling caste. It expanded into a secret society, always with its headquarters here in this city. It soon became Moslem, a clan of fanatical haters of the Feringi, and the emirs sold the swords of their followers to many leaders of jihad, the holy war.

"It flourished, then decayed. A hundred years ago the clan was nearly exterminated in a hill feud, and the organization became a shadow, limited to the rulers and officials of Rub el Harami alone. But they still held the city. Ten years ago I cut loose from my people and became a Moslem, heart and soul. In my wanderings I discovered the Black Tigers, and saw their potentialities. I journeyed to Rub el Harami, and here I stumbled upon a secret that set my brain on fire.

"But I run ahead of my tale. It was only three years ago that I gained admittance into the clan. It was during the seven years preceding that, seven years of wandering, fighting, and plotting all over Asia, that clashed more than once with El Borak, and learned how dangerous the man was—and that we must always be enemies, since our interests and ideals were so antithetical. So when I came to Rub el Harami, I simply dropped out of sight of El Borak and all the other adventurers that like him and me rove the waste places of the East. Before I came to the city, I spent months in erasing my tracks. Valdimir Jakrovitch, known also as Akbar Shah, disappeared entirely. Not even El Borak connected him with Abd el Khafid, wanderer from Samarkand. I had stepped into a completely new rôle and personality. If El Borak should see me, he might suspect—but he never shall, except as my captive.

"Without interference from him I began to build up the clan, first as a member of the ranks, from which I swiftly rose, then as prince of the clan, to which position I attained less than a year ago, by means and intrigues I shall not inflict upon you. I have reorganized the society, expanded it as of old, placed my spies in every country in the world. Of course El Borak must have heard that the Black Tiger was stirring again; but to him it would mean only the spasmodic activity of a band of fanatics, without international significance.

"But he would guess its true meaning if he knew that Abd el Khafid is the man he fought up and down the length and breadth of Asia, years ago!" The man's eyes blazed, his voice vibrated. In his super-egotism he found intense satisfaction in even so small and hostile an audience as his prisoner. "Did you ever hear of the Golden Cave of Shaitan el Kabir?

"It lies within a day's ride of the city, so carefully hidden that an army of men might search for it forever, in vain. But I have seen it! It is a sight to madden a man— heaped from floor to roof with blocks of gold! It is the offerings to Shaitan—custom dating from old heathen days. Each year a hundred-weight of gold, levied on the people of the city, is melted and molded in small blocks, and carried and placed in the cave by the imams and the emir. And—"

"Do you mean to tell me that a treasure of that size exists near this city of thieves?" demanded Brent incredulously.

"Why not? Have you not heard the city's customs are unbending as iron? Only the imams know the secret of the cave; the knowledge is handed down from imam to imam, from emir to emir. The people do not know; they suppose the gold is taken by Shaitan to his infernal abode. If they knew, they would not touch it. Take gold dedicated the Shaitan the Damned? You little know the Oriental mind. Not a Moselm in the world would touch a grain of it, even though he were starving.

"But I am free of such superstitions. Within a few days the gift to Shaitan will be placed in the cave. It will be another year then before the imams visit the cavern again. And before that time comes around, I will have accomplished my purpose. I will secretly remove the gold from the cave, working utterly alone, and will melt it down and recast it in different forms. Oh, I understand the art and have the proper equipment. When I have finished, none can recognize it as the accursed gold of Shaitan.

"With it I can feed and equip an army! I can buy rifles, ammunition, machine guns, airplanes, and mercenaries to fly them. I can arm every cutthroat in the Himalayas! These hill tribes have the makings of the finest army in the world—all they need is equipment. And that equipment I will supply. There are plenty of European sources ready to sell me whatever I want. And the gold of Shaitan will supply my needs!" The man was sweating, his eyes blazing as if madness like molten gold had entered his veins. "The world never dreamed of such a treasure-trove! The golden offerings of a thousand years heaped from floor to ceiling! And it is *mine!*"

"The imams will kill you!" whispered Brent, appalled.

"They will not know for nearly a year. I will invent a lie to explain my great wealth. They will not suspect until they open the cave next year. Then it will be too late. Then I will be free from the Black Tigers. I will be an emperor!

"With my great new army I will sweep down into the plains of India. I will lead a horde of Afghans, Persians, Pathans, Arabs, Turkomen that will make up for discipline by numbers and ferocity. The Indian Moslems will rise! I will sweep the English out of the land! I will rule supreme from Samarkand to Cape Comorin!"

"Why do you tell me this?" asked Brent. "What's to prevent me from betraying you to the imams?"

"You will never see an imam," was the grim reply. "I will see that you have no opportunity to talk. But enough of this: I allowed you to come alive to Rub el Harami only because I wanted to learn what secret password Stockton gave you to use with the British officials. I know you had one, by the speed and ease with which you were passed up to Kabul. I have long sought to get one of my spies into the very vitals of the secret service. This password will enable me to do so. Tell me what it is."

Brent laughed sardonically, then. "You're going to kill me anyway. I certainly don't intend to deprive myself of this one tiny crumb of retaliation. I'm not going to put another weapon in your filthy hands."

"You're a fool!" exclaimed Abd el Khafid, with a flash of anger too sudden, too easily aroused for complete self-confidence. The man was on edge, and not so sure of himself as he seemed.

"Doubtless," agreed Brent tranquilly. "And what about it?"

"Very well!" Abd el Khafid restrained himself by an obvious effort. "I cannot touch you to-night. You are the property of the city, according to age-old custom not even I can ignore. But to-morrow you will be sold on the block to the highest bidder. No one wants a Feringi slave, except for the pleasure of torturing. They are too soft for hard work. I will buy you for a few rupees, and then there will be nothing to prevent my *making* you talk. Before I fling your mangled carcass out on the garbage heap for the vultures, you will have told me everything I want to know."

Abruptly he turned and stalked out of the dungeon. Brent heard his footsteps reëcho hollowly on the flags of the corridor. A wisp of conversation came back faintly. Then a door slammed and there was nothing but silence and a star blinking dimly through the barred window.

In another part of the city Shirkuh lounged on a silken divan, under the glow of bronze lamps that struck sparkling glints from the rich wine brimming in golden goblets. Shirkuh drank deep, smacking his lips, desert-fashion, as a matter of politeness to his host. He seemed to have no thought in the world except the quenching of his thirst, but Alafdal Khan, on another couch, knit his brows in perplexity. He was uncovering astonishing discoveries in this wild young warrior from the western mountains—unsuspected subtleties and hidden depths.

"Why do you wish to buy this *Melakani?*" he damanded.

"He is necessary to us," asserted Shirkuh. With the bronze lamps throwing his face into half shadow, the boyishness was gone, replaced by a keen hawklike hardness and maturity.

"We must have him. I will buy him in the *suk* tomorrow, and he will aid us in making you emir of Rub el Harami."

"But you have no money!" expostulated the Waziri.

"You must lend it to me."

"But Abd el Khafid desires him," argued Alafdal Khan. "He sent Muhammad ez Zahir out to capture him. It would be unwise to bid against the emir."

Shirkuh emptied his cup before answering.

"From what you have told me of the city," he said presently, "this is the situation. Only a certain per cent of the citizens are Black Tigers. They constitute a ruling caste and a sort of police force to support the emir. The emirs are complete despots, except when checked by customs whose roots are lost in the mists of antiquity. They rule with an iron rein over a turbulent and lawless population, composed of the dregs and scum of Central Asia."

"That is true," agreed Alafdal Khan.

"But in the past, the people have risen and deposed a ruler who trampled on tradition, forcing the Black Tigers to elevate another prince. Very well. You have told me that the number of Black Tigers in the city is comparatively small at present. Many have been sent as spies or emissaries to other regions. You yourself are high in the ranks of the clan."

"An empty honor," said Alafdal bitterly. "My advice is never asked in council. I have no authority except with my own personal retainers. And they are less than those of Abd el Khafid or Ali Shah."

"It is upon the crowd in the streets we must rely," replied Shirkuh. "You are popular with the masses. They are almost ready to rise under you, were you to declare yourself. But that will come later. They need a leader and a motive. We will supply both. But first we must secure the Feringi. With him safe in our hands, we will plan our next move in the game."

Alafdal Khan scowled, his powerful fingers knotting about the slender stem of the wineglass. Conflicting emotions of vanity, ambition, and fear played across his broad face.

"You talk high!" he complained. "You ride into Rub el Harami, a penniless adventurer, and say you can make me emir of the city! How do I know you are not an empty bag of wind? How can you make me prince of Rub el Harami?"

Shirkuh set down his wineglass and rose, folding his arms. He looked somberly down at the astounded Waziri, all naïveness and reckless humor gone out of his face. He spoke a single phrase, and Alafdal ejaculated stranglingly and lurched to his feet, spilling his wine. He reeled like a drunkard, clutching at the divan, his dilated eyes searching, with a fierce intensity, the dark, immobile face before him.

"Do you believe, now, that I can make you emir of Rub el Harami?" demanded Shirkuh.

"Who could doubt it?" panted Alafdal. "Have you not put kings on their thrones? But you are mad, to come here! One word to the mob and they would rend you limb from limb!"

"You will not speak that word," said Shirkuh with conviction. "You will not throw away the lordship of Rub el Harami."

And Alafdal nodded slowly, the fire of ambition surging redly in his eyes.

CHAPTER V.

Swords in the "Suk"

DAWN STREAMING GRAYLY through the barred window
awakened Brent. He reflected that it might be the last
dawn he would see as a free man. He laughed wryly at the
thought. Free? Yet at least he was still a captive, not a
slave. There was a vast difference between a captive and a
slave—a revolting gulf, in which, crossing, a man or
woman's self-respect must be forever lost.

Presently black slaves came with a jug of cheap sour
wine, and food—chupatties, rice cakes, dried dates.
Royal fare compared with his supper the night before. A
Tajik barber shaved him and trimmed his hair, and he was
allowed the luxury of scrubbing himself pink in the prison
bath.

He was grateful for the opportunity, but the whole
proceeding was disgusting. He felt like a prize animal
being curried and groomed for display. Some whim
prompted him to ask the barber where the proceeds of his
sale would go, and the man answered into the city
treasury, to keep the walls repaired. A singularly
unromantic usage for the price of a human being, but

typical of the hard practicality of the East. Brent thought
fleetingly of Shirkuh, then shrugged his shoulders.
Apparently the Kurd had abandoned him to his fate.

Clad only in a loin cloth and sandals, he was led from
the prison by the one-eyed Sudozai and a huge black
slave. Horses were waiting for them at the gate, and he
was ordered to mount. Between the slave masters he
clattered up the street before the sun was up. But already
the crowd was gathering in the square. The auctioning of
a white man was an event, and there was, furthermore, a
feeling of expectancy in the air, sharpened by the fight of
the day before.

In the midst of the square there stood a thick platform
built solidly of stone blocks; it was perhaps four feet high
and thirty feet across. On this platform the Sudozai took
his stand, grasping a piece of rope which was tied loosely
about Brent's neck. Behind them stood the stolid
Soudanese with a drawn scimitar on his shoulder.

Before, and to one side of the block the crowd had left a
space clear, and there Abd el Khafid sat his horse, amid a
troop of Black Tigers, bizarre in their ceremonial armor.
Ceremonial it must be, reflected Brent; it might turn a
sword blade, but it would afford no protection against a
bullet. But it was one of the many fantastic customs of the
city, where tradition took the place of written law. The
bodyguard of the emir had always worn black armor.
Therefore, they would always wear it. Muhammad ez
Zahir commanded them. Brent did not see Ali Shah.

Another custom was responsible for the presence of
Abd el Khafid, instead of sending a servant to buy the
American for him; not even the emir could bid by proxy.

As he climbed upon the block, Brent heard a cheer, and
saw Alafdal Khan and Shirkuh pushing through the
throng on their horses. Behind them came thirty-five
warriors, well armed and well mounted. The Waziri chief
was plainly nervous, but Shirkuh strutted like a peacock,
even on horseback, before the admiring gaze of the
throng.

At the ringing ovation given them, annoyance flitted

across Abd el Khafid's broad, pale face, and that
expression was followed by a more sinister darkening that
boded ill for the Waziri and his ally.

The auction began abruptly and undramatically. The
Sudozai began in a singsong voice to narrate the desirable
physical points of the prisoner, when Abd el Khafid cut
him short and offered fifty rupees.

"A hundred!" instantly yelled Shirkuh.

Abd el Khafid turned an irritated and menacing glare
on him. Shirkuh grinned insolently, and the crowd
hugged itself, sensing a conflict of the sort it loved.

"Three hundred!" snarled the emir, meaning to squelch
this irreverent vagabond without delay.

"Four hundred!" shouted Shirkuh.

"A thousand!" cried Adb el Khafid in a passion.

"Eleven hundred!"

And Shirkuh deliberately laughed in the emir's face,
and the crowd laughed with him. Abd el Khafid appeared
at a disadvantage, for he was a bit confused at this
unexpected opposition, and had lost his temper too
easily. The fierce eyes of the crowd missed nothing of this,
for it is on such points the wolf pack ceaselessly and
pitilessly judges its leader. Their sympathies swung to the
laughing, youthful stranger, sitting his horse with careless
ease.

Brent's heart had leaped into his throat at the first
sound of Shirkuh's voice. If the man meant to aid him,
this was the most obvious way to take. Then his heart
sank again at the determination in Abd el Khafid's angry
face. The emir would never let his captive slip between his
fingers. And though the Gift of Shaitan was not yet in the
Russian's possession, yet doubtless his private resources
were too great for Shirkuh. In a contest of finances
Shirkuh was foredoomed to lose.

Brent's conclusions were not those of Abd el Khafid.
The emir shot a glance at Alafdal Khan, shifting uneasily
in his saddle. He saw the beads of moisture gathered on
the Waziri's broad brow, and realized a collusion between

the men. New anger blazed in the emir's eyes.

In his way Abd el Khafid was miserly. He was willing to squander gold like water on a main objective, but it irked him exceedingly to pay an exorbitant price to attain a minor goal. He knew—every man in the crowd knew now—that Alafdal Khan was backing Shirkuh. And all men knew that the Waziri was one of the wealthiest men in the city, and a prodigal spender. Abd el Khafid's nostrils pinched in with wrath as he realized the heights of extravagance to which he might be forced, did Shirkuh persist in this impertinent opposition to his wishes. The Gift of Shaitan was not yet in his hands, and his private funds were drained constantly by the expenses of his spy system and his various intrigues. He raised the bid in a harsh, anger-edged voice.

Brent, studying the drama with the keen, understanding eyes of a gambler, realized that Abd el Khafid had got off on the wrong foot. Shirkuh's bearing appealed to the crowd. They laughed at his sallies, which were salty and sparkling with all the age-old ribaldry of the East, and they hissed covertly at the emir, under cover of their neighbors.

The bidding mounted to unexpected heights. Abd el Khafid, white about the nostrils as he sensed the growing hostility of the crowd, did not speak except to snarl his offers. Shirkuh rolled in his saddle, slapped his thighs, yelled his bids, and defiantly brandished a leathern bag which gave out a musical tinkling.

The excitement of the crowd was at white heat. Ferocity began to edge their yells. Brent, looking down at the heaving mass, had a confused impression of dark, convulsed faces, blazing eyes, and strident voices. Alafdal Khan was sweating, but he did not interfere, not even when the bidding rose above fifty thousand rupees.

It was more than a bidding contest; it was the subtle play of two opposing wills, as hard and supple as tempered steel. Abd el Khafid realized that if he withdrew now, his prestige would never recover from the blow. In his rage he made his first mistake.

He rose suddenly in his stirrups, clapping his hands.

"Let there be an end to this madness!" he roared. "No white slave is worth this much! I declare the auction closed! I buy this dog for sixty thousand rupees! Take him to my house, slave master!"

A roar of protest rose from the throng, and Shirkuh drove his horses alongside the block and leaped off to it, tossing his rein to a Waziri.

"Is this justice?" he shouted. "Is this done according to custom? Men of Rub el Harami, I demand justice! I bid sixty-one thousand rupees. I stand ready to bid more, if necessary! When has an emir been allowed to use his authority to rob a citizen, and cheat the people? Nay, we be thieves—but shall we rob one another? Who is Abd el Khafid, to trample the customs of the city! If the customs are broken, what shall hold you together? Rub el Harami lives only so long as the ancient traditions are observed. Will you let Abd el Khafid destroy them—and you?"

A cataract of straining human voices answered him. The crowd had become a myriad-fanged, flashing-eyed mass of hate.

"Obey the customs!" yelled Shirkuh, and the crowd took up the yell.

"*Obey the customs!*" It was the thunder of unreined seas, the roar of a storm wind ripping through icy passes. Blindly men seized the slogan, yowling it under a forest of lean arms and clenched fists. Men go mad on a slogan; conquerors have swept to empire, prophets to new world religions on a shouted phrase. All the men in the square were screaming it like a ritual now, rocking and tossing on their feet, fists clenched, froth on their lips. They no longer reasoned; they were a forest of blind human emotions, swayed by the storm wind of a shouted phrase that embodied passion and the urge to action.

Abd el Khafid lost his head. He drew his sword and cut a man who was clawing at his stirrup mouthing: "Obey the customs, emir!" and the spurt of blood edged the yells with murder lust. But as yet the mob was only a blind, raging monster without a head.

"Clear the *suk!*" shouted Abd el Khafid.

The lances dipped, and the Black Tigers moved forward uncertainly. A hail of stones greeted them.

Shirkuh leaped to the edge of the block, lifting his arms, shouting, cutting the volume of sound by the knifing intensity of his yell.

"Down with Abd el Khafid! Hail, Alafdal Khan, emir of Rub el Harami!"

"Hail, Alafdal Khan!" came back from the crowd like a thunderclap.

Abd el Khafid rose in his stirrups, livid.

"Fools! Are you utterly mad? Shall I call my riders to sweep the streets clear of you?"

Shirkuh threw back his head and laughed like a wolf howling.

"Call them!" he yelled. "Before you can gather them from the taverns and dens, we will stain the square with your blood! Prove your right to rule! You have violated one custom—redeem yourself by another! Men of Rub el Harami, is it not a tradition that an emir must be able to defend his title with the sword?"

"Aye!" roared back the mob.

"Then let Abd el Khafid fight Alafdal Khan!" shouted Shirkuh.

"Let them fight!" bellowed the mob.

Abd el Khafid's eyes turned red. He was sure of his prowess with the sword, but this revolt against his authority enraged him to the point of insanity. This was the very center of his power; here like a spider he had spun his webs, expecting attack on the fringes, but never here. Now he was caught off-guard. Too many trusted henchmen were far afield. Others were scattered throughout the city, useless to him at the moment. His bodyguard was too small to defy the crowd. Mentally he promised himself a feast of hangings and beheadings when he could bring back a sufficient force of men to Rub el Harami. In the meantime he would settle Alafdal's ambitions permanently.

"Kingmaker, eh?" he snarled in Shirkuh's face, as he leaped off his horse to the block. He whipped out his

tulwar and swung it around his head, a sheen of silver in
the sun. "I'll nail your head to the Herati Gate when I've
finished with this ox-eyed fool!"

Shirkuh laughed at him and stepped back, herding the
slave masters and their captive to the back of the block.
Alafdal Khan was scrambling to the platform, his tulwar
in his hand.

He was not fully straightened on the block when Abd el
Khafid was on him with the fury of a tornado. The crowd
cried out, fearing that the emir's whirlwind speed would
envelop the powerful but slower chief. But it was this very
swiftness that undid the Russian. In his wild fury to kill,
Abd el Khafid forgot judgment. The stroke he aimed at
Alafdal's head would have decapitated an ox; but he
began it in mid-stride, and its violence threw his
descending foot out of line. He stumbled, his blade cut
thin air as Alafdal dodged—and then the Waziri's sword
was through him.

It was over in a flash. Abd el Khafid had practically
impaled himself on the Waziri's blade. The rush, the
stroke, the counter-thrust, and the emir kicking his life
out on the stone like a spitted rat—it all happened in a
mere tick of time that left the mob speechless.

Shirkuh sprang forward like a panther in the instant of
silence while the crowd held its breath and Alafdal gaped
stupidly from the red tulwar in his hand to the dead man
at his feet.

"Hail to Alafdal Khan, emir of Rub el Harami!" yelled
Shirkuh, and the crowd thundered its response.

"On your horse, man, quick!" Shirkuh snarled in
Alafdal's ear, thrusting him toward his steed, while
seeming to bow him toward it.

The crowd was going mad with the senseless joy of a
mob that sees its favorite elevated above them. As
Alafdal, still dazed by the rapidity of events, clambered
on his horse, Shirkuh turned on the stunned Black Tiger
riders.

"Dogs!" he thundered. "Form ranks! Escort your new

master to the palace, for his title to be confirmed by the council of imams!"

They were moving unwillingly forward, afraid of the crowd, when a commotion interrupted the flow of events. Ali Shah and forty armed horsemen came pushing their way through the crowd and halted beside the armored riders. The crowd bared its teeth, remembering the Ghilzai's feud with their new emir. Yet there was iron in Ali Shah. He did not flinch, but the old indecision wavered in Alafdal's eyes at the sight of his foe.

Shirkuh turned on Ali Shah with the swift suspicion of a tiger, but before anyone could speak, a wild figure dashed from among the Ghilzais and leaped on the block. It was the Shinwari Shirkuh had ridden down the day before. The man threw a lean arm out toward Shirkuh.

"He is an impostor, brothers!" he screamed. "I thought I knew him yesterday! An hour ago I remembered! He is no Kurd! He is—"

Shirkuh shot the man through the body. He staggered to a rolling fall that carried him to the edge of the block. There he lifted himself on an elbow, and pointed at Shirkuh. Blood spattered the Shinwari's beard as he croaked in the sudden silence:

"I swear by the beard of the Prophet, he is no Moslem! *He is El Borak!*"

A shudder passed over the crowd.

"Obey the customs!" came Ali Shah's sardonic voice in the unnatural stillness. "You killed your emir because of a small custom. There stands a man who has violated the greatest one—your enemy, El Borak!"

There was conviction in his voice, yet no one had really doubted the accusation of the dying Shinwari. The amazing revelation had struck them all dumb, Brent included. But only for an instant.

The blind reaction of the crowd was as instantaneous as it had been before. The tense stillness snapped like a banjo string to a flood of sound:

"Down with the infidels! Death to El Borak! Death to Alafdal Khan!"

• • •

To Brent it seemed that the crowd suddenly rose like a
foaming torrent and flowed over the edge of the block.
Above the deafening clamor he heard the crashing of the
big automatic in El Borak's hand. Blood spattered, and in
an instant the edge of the block was littered by writhing
bodies over which the living tripped and stumbled.

El Borak sprang to Brent, knocked his guards
sprawling with the pistol barrel, and seized the dazed
captive, dragged him toward the black stallion to which
the Waziri still clung. The mob was swarming like wolves
about Alafdal and his warriors, and the Black Tigers and
Ali Shah were trying to get at them through the press.
Alafdal bawled something desperate and incoherent to El
Borak as he laid lustily about him with his tulwar. The
Waziri chief was almost crazed with bewilderment. A
moment ago he had been emir of Rub el Harami, with the
crowd applauding him. Now the same crowd was trying
to take him out of his saddle.

"Make for your house, Alafdal!" yelled El Borak.

He leaped into the saddle just as the man holding the
horse went down with his head shattered by a cobble-
stone. The wild figure who had killed him leaped forward,
gibbering, clawing at the rider's leg. El Borak drove a
sharp silver heel into his eye, stretching him bleeding and
screaming on the ground. He ruthlessly slashed off a hand
that grasped at his rein, and beat back a ring of snarling
faces with another swing of his saber.

"Get on behind me, Brent!" he ordered, holding the
frantic horse close to the block.

It was only when he heard the English words, with their
Southwestern accent, that Brent realized that this was no
dream, and he had at last actually encountered the man he
had sought.

Men were grasping at Brent. He beat them off with
clenched fists, leaped on the stallion behind the saddle. He
grasped the cantle, resisting the natural impulse to hold
onto the man in front of him. El Borak would need the

free use of his body if they won through that seething mass of frantic humanity which packed the square from edge to edge. It was a frothing, dark-waved sea, swirling about islands of horsemen.

But the stallion gathered itself and lunged terribly, knocking over screaming figures like tenpins. Bones snapped under its hoofs. Over the heads of the crowd Brent saw Ali Shah and his riders beating savagely at the mob with their swords, trying to reach Alafdal Khan. Ali Shah was cool no longer; his dark face was convulsed.

The stallion waded through that sea of humanity, its rider slashing right and left, clearing a red road. Brent felt hands clawing at them as they went by, felt the inexorable hoofs grinding over writhing bodies. Ahead of them the Waziris, in a compact formation, were cutting their way toward the west side of the square. Already a dozen of them had been dragged from their saddles and torn to pieces.

El Borak dragged his rifle out of its boot, and it banged redly in the snarling faces, blasting a lane through them. Along that lane the black stallion thundered, to smite with irresistible impact the mass hemming in Alafdal Khan. It burst asunder, and the black horse sped on, while its rider yelled:

"Fall in behind me! We'll make a stand at your house!"

The Waziris closed in behind him. They might have abandoned El Borak if they had had the choice. But the people included them all in their blind rage against the breakers of tradition. As they broke through the press, behind them the Black Tigers brought their rifles into play for the first time. A hail of bullets swept the square, emptying half the Waziri saddles. The survivors dashed into a narrow street.

A mass of snarling figures blocked their way. Men swarmed from the houses to cut them off. Men were surging into the alley behind them. A thrown stone numbed Brent's shoulder. El Borak was using the empty rifle like a mace. In a rush they smote the men massed in the street.

The great black stallion reared and lashed down with malletlike hoofs, and its rider flailed with a rifle stock now splintered and smeared with blood. But behind them Alafdal's steed stumbled and fell. Alafdal's disordered turban and his dripping tulwar appeared for an instant above a sea of heads and tossing arms. His men plunged madly in to rescue him and were hemmed in by a solid mass of humanity as more men surged down the street from the square. Hamstrung horses went down, screaming. El Borak wheeled his stallion back toward the mêlée, and as he did so, a swarm of men burst from a narrow alleyway. One seized Brent's leg and dragged him from the horse. As they rolled in the dust, the Afghan heaved Brent below him, mouthing like an ape, and lifted a crooked knife. Brent saw it glint in the sunlight, had an instant's numb realization of doom—then El Borak, reining the rearing stallion around, leaned from the saddle and smashed the Afghan's skull with his rifle butt.

The man fell across Brent, and then from an arched doorway an ancient blunderbuss banged, and the stallion reared and fell sprawling, half its head shot away. El Borak leaped clear, hit on his feet like a cat, and hurled the broken rifle in the faces of the swarm bearing down on him. He leaped back, tearing his saber clear. It flickered like lightning, and three men fell with cleft heads. But the mob was blood-mad, heedless of death. Brainlessly they rushed against him, flailing with staves and bludgeons, bearing him by their very weight back into an arched doorway. The panels splintered inward under the impact of the hurtling bodies, and El Borak vanished from Brent's sight. The mob poured in after him.

Brent cast off the limp body that lay across him and rose. He had a brief glimpse of a dark writhing mass where the fight swirled about the fallen chief, of Ali Shah and his riders beating at the crowd with their swords— then a bludgeon, wielded from behind, fell glancingly on his head, and he fell blind and senseless into the trampled dust.

● ● ●

Slowly consciousness returned to Stuart Brent. His head ached dully, and his hair was stiff with clotted blood. He struggled to his elbows, though the effort made his head swim sickeningly, and stared about him.

He was lying on a stone floor littered with moldy straw. Light came in from a high-barred window. There was a door with a broad barred wicket. Other figures lay near him and one sat cross-legged, staring at him blankly. It was Alafdal Khan.

The Waziri's beard was torn, his turban gone. His features were swollen, and bruised, and skinned, one ear mangled. Three of his men lay near, one groaning. All had been frightfully beaten, and the man who groaned seemed to have a broken arm.

"They didn't kill us!" marveled Brent.

Alafdal Khan swung his great head like an ox in pain and groaned: "Cursed be the day I laid eyes on El Borak!"

One of the men crept painfully to Brent's side.

"I am Achmet, sahib," he said, spitting blood from a broken tooth. "There lie Hassan and Suleiman. Ali Shah and his men beat the dogs off us, but they had mauled us so that all were dead save these you see. Our lord is like one touched by Allah."

"Are we in the Abode of the Damned?" asked Brent.

"Nay, sahib. We are in the common jail which lies near the west wall."

"Why did they save us from the mob?"

"For a more exquisite end!" Achmet shuddered. "Does the sahib know the death the Black Tigers reserve for traitors?"

"No!" Brent's lips were suddenly dry.

"We will be flayed to-morrow night in the square. It is an old pagan custom. Rub El Harami is a city of customs."

"So I have learned!" agreed Brent grimly. "What of El Borak?"

"I do not know. He vanished into a house, with many men in pursuit. They must have overtaken and slain him."

CHAPTER VI.

The Executioner

WHEN THE DOOR in the archway burst inward under the impact of Gordon's iron-hard shoulders, he tumbled backward into a dim, carpeted hallway. His pursuers, crowding after him, jammed in the doorway in a sweating, cursing crush which his saber quickly turned into a shambles. Before they could clear the door of the dead, he was racing down the hall.

He made a turn to the left, ran across a chamber where veiled women squealed and scattered, emerged into a narrow alley, leaped a low wall, and found himself in a small garden. Behind him sounded the clamor of his hunters, momentarily baffled. He crossed the garden and through a partly open door came into a winding corridor. Somewhere a slave was singing in the weird chant of the Soudan, apparently heedless of the dog-fight noises going on upon the other side of the wall. Gordon moved down the corridor, careful to keep his silver heels from clinking. Presently he came to a winding staircase and up it he went, making no noise on the richly carpeted steps. As he came out into an upper corridor, he saw a curtained door and heard beyond it a faint, musical clinking which he recognized. He glided to the partly open door and peered through the curtains. In a richly appointed room, lighted by a tinted skylight, a portly, gray-bearded man sat with his back to the door, counting coins out of a leather bag into an ebony chest. He was so intent on the business at hand that he did not seem aware of the growing clamor below. Or perhaps street riots were too common in Rub el Harami to attract the attention of a thrifty merchant, intent only on increasing his riches.

Pad of swift feet on the stair, and Gordon slipped behind the partly open door. A richly clad young man, with a scimitar in his hand, ran up the steps and hurried to the door. He thrust the curtains aside and paused on the threshold, panting with haste and excitement.

"Father!" he shouted. "El Borak is in the city! Do you not hear the din below? They are hunting him through the houses! He may be in our very house! Men are searching the lower rooms even now!"

"Let them hunt him," replied the old man. "Remain here with me, Abdullah. Shut that door and lock it. El Borak is a tiger."

As the youth turned, instead of the yielding curtain behind him, he felt the contact of a hard, solid body, and simultaneously a corded arm locked about his neck, choking his startled cry. Then he felt the light prick of a knife and he went limp with fright, his scimitar sliding from his nerveless hand. The old man had turned at his son's gasp, and now he froze, gray beneath his beard, his moneybag dangling.

Gordon thrust the youth into the room, not releasing his grip, and let the curtains close behind them.

"Do not move," he warned the old man softly.

He dragged his trembling captive across the room and into a tapestried alcove. Before he vanished into it, he spoke briefly to the merchant:

"They are coming up the stairs, looking for me. Meet them at the door and send them away. Do not play me false by even the flick of an eyelash, if you value your son's life."

The old man's eyes were dilated with pure horror. Gordon well knew the power of paternal affection. In a welter of hate, treachery, and cruelty, it was a real and vital passion, as strong as the throb of the human heart. The merchant might defy Gordon were his own life alone at stake; but the American knew he would not risk the life of his son.

Sandals stamped up the stair, and rough voices shouted. The old man hurried to the door, stumbling in his haste. He thrust his head through the curtains, in response to a bawled question. His reply came plainly to Gordon.

"El Borak? Dogs! Take your clamor from my walls! If El Borak is in the house of Nureddin el Aziz, he is in the rooms below. Ye have searched them? Then look for him elsewhere, and a curse on you!"

The footsteps dwindled down the stair, the voices faded and ceased.

Gordon pushed Abdullah out into the chamber.

"Shut the door!" the American ordered.

Nureddin obeyed, with poisonous eyes but fear-twisted face.

"I will stay in this room a while," said Gordon. "If you play me false—if any man besides yourself crosses that threshold, the first stroke of the fight will plunge my blade in Abdullah's heart."

"What do you wish?" asked Nureddin nervously.

"Give me the key to that door. No, toss it on the table there. Now go forth into the streets and learn if the Feringi, or any of the Waziris live. Then return to me. And if you love your son, keep my secret!"

The merchant left the room without a word, and Gordon bound Abdullah's wrists and ankles with strips torn from the curtains. The youth was gray with fear, incapable of resistance. Gordon laid him on a divan, and reloaded his big automatic. He discarded the tattered remnants of his robe. The white silk shirt beneath was torn, revealing his muscular breast, his close-fitting breeches smeared with blood.

Nureddin returned presently, rapping at the door and naming himself.

Gordon unlocked the door and stepped back, his pistol muzzle a few inches from Abdullah's ear. But the old man was alone when he hurried in. He closed the door and sighed with relief to see Abdullah uninjured.

"What is your news?" demanded Gordon.

"Men comb the city for you, and Ali Shah has declared himself prince of the Black Tigers. The imams have confirmed his claim. The mob has looted Alafdal Khan's house and slain every Waziri they could find. But the Feringi lives, and so likewise does Alafdal Khan and three of his men. They lie in the common jail. To-morrow night they die."

"Do your slaves suspect my presence?"

"Nay. None saw you enter."

"Good. Bring wine and food. Abdullah shall taste it before I eat."

"My slaves will think it strange to see me bearing food!"

"Go to the stair and call your orders down to them. Bid them set the food outside the door and then return downstairs."

This was done, and Gordon ate and drank heartily, sitting cross-legged on the divan at Abdullah's head, his pistol on his lap.

The day wore on. El Borak sat motionless, his eternal vigilance never relaxing. The Afghans watched him, hating and fearing him. As evening approached, he spoke to Nureddin after a silence that had endured for hours.

"Go and procure for me a robe and cloak of black silk, and a black helmet such as is worn by the Black Tigers. Bring me also boots with lower heels than these—and not silver—and a mask such as members of the clan wear on secret missions."

The old man frowned. "The garments I can procure

from my own shop. But how am I to secure the helmet and mask?"

"That is thy affair. Gold can open any door, they say. Go!"

As soon as Nureddin had departed, reluctantly, Gordon kicked off his boots, and next removed his mustache, using the keen-edged dagger for a razor. With its removal vanished the last trace of Shirkuh the Kurd.

Twilight had come to Rub el Harami. The room seemed full of a blue mist, blurring objects. Gordon had lighted a bronze lamp when Nureddin returned with the articles El Borak had ordered.

"Lay them on the table and sit down on the divan with your hands behind you," Gordon commanded.

When the merchant had done so, the American bound his wrists and ankles. Then Gordon donned the boots and the robe, placed the black lacquered steel helmet on his head, and drew the black cloak about him; lastly he put on the mask which fell in folds of black silk to his breast, with two slits over his eyes. Turning to Nureddin, he asked:

"Is there a likeness between me and another?"

"Allah preserve us! You are one with Dhira Azrail, the executioner of the Black Tigers, when he goes forth to slay at the emir's command."

"Good. I have heard much of this man who slays secretly, who moves through the night like a black jinn of destruction. Few have seen his face, men say."

"Allah defend me from ever seeing it!" said Nureddin fervently.

Gordon glanced at the skylight. Stars twinkled beyond it.

"I go now from your house, Nureddin," said he. "But lest you rouse the household in your zeal of hospitality, I must gag you and your son."

"We will smother!" exclaimed Nureddin. "We will starve in this room!"

"You will do neither one nor the other," Gordon assured him. "No man I gagged ever smothered. Has not Allah given you nostrils through which to breathe? Your servants will find you and release you in the morning."

This was deftly accomplished, and Gordon advised:

"Observe that I have not touched your moneybags, and be grateful!"

He left the room, locking the door behind him. He hoped it would be several hours before either of his captives managed to work the gag out of his mouth and arouse the household with his yells.

Moving like a black-clad ghost through the dimly lighted corridors, Gordon descended the winding stair and came into the lower hallway. A black slave sat cross-legged at the foot of the stair, but his head was sunk on his broad breast, and his snores resounded through the hall. He did not see or hear the velvet-footed shadow that glided past him. Gordon slid back the bolt on the door and emerged into the garden, whose broad leaves and petals hung motionless in the still starlight. Outside, the city was silent. Men had gone early behind locked doors, and few roamed the streets, except those patrols searching ceaselessly for El Borak.

He climbed the wall and dropped into the narrow alley. He knew where the common jail was, for in his rôle of Shirkuh he had familiarized himself with the general features of the town. He kept close to the wall, under the shadows of the overhanging balconies, but he did not slink. His movements were calculated to suggest a man who has no reason for concealment, but who chooses to shun conspicuousness.

The street seemed empty. From some of the roof gardens came the wail of native citterns, or voices lifted in song. Somewhere a wretch sereamed agonizingly to the impact of blows on naked flesh.

Once Gordon heard the clink of steel ahead of him and turned quickly into a dark alley to let a patrol swing past. They were men in armor, on foot, but carrying cocked rifles at the ready and peering in every direction. They kept close together, and their vigilance reflected their fear of the quarry they hunted. When they rounded the first corner, he emerged from his hiding place and hurried on.

But he had to depend on his disguise before he reached the prison. A squad of armed men rounded the corner ahead of him, and no concealment offered itself. At the sound of their footsteps he had slowed his pace to a stately stride. With his cloak folded close about him, his head slightly bent as if in somber meditation, he moved on, paying no heed to the soldiers. They shrank back, murmuring:

"Allah preserve us! It is Dhira Azrail—the Arm of the Angel of Death! An order has been given!"

They hurried on, without looking back. A few moments later Gordon had reached the lowering arch of the prison door. A dozen guardsmen stood alertly under the arch, their rifle barrels gleaming bluely in the glare of a torch thrust in a niche in the wall. These rifles were instantly leveled at the figure that moved out of the shadows. Then the men hesitated, staring wide-eyed at the somber black shape standing silently before them.

"Your pardon!" entreated the captain of the guard, saluting. "We could not recognize—in the shadow—We did not know an order had been given."

A ghostly hand, half muffled in the black cloak, gestured toward the door, and the guardsmen opened it in stumbling haste, salaaming deeply. As the black figure moved through, they closed the door and made fast the chain.

"The mob will see no show in the *suk* after all," muttered one.

CHAPTER VII.

In The Prison

IN THE CELL where Brent and his companions lay, time dragged on leaden feet. Hassan groaned with the pain of his broken arm. Suleiman cursed Ali Shah in a monotonous drone. Achmet was inclined to talk, but his comments cast no light of hope on their condition. Alafdal Khan sat like a man in a daze.

No food was given them, only scummy water that smelled. They used most of it to bathe their wounds. Brent suggested trying to set Hassan's arm, but the others showed no interest. Hassan had only another day to live. Why bother? Then there was nothing with which to make splints.

Brent mostly lay on his back, watching the little square of dry blue Himalayan sky through the barred window.

He watched the blue fade, turn pink with sunset and deep purple with twilight; it became a square of blue-black velvet, set with a cluster of white stars. Outside, in the corridor that ran between the cells, bronze lamps glowed, and he wondered vaguely how far, on the backs of groaning camels, had come the oil that filled them.

In their light a cloaked figure came down the corridor, and a scarred sardonic face was pressed to the bars. Achmet gasped, his eyes dilated.

"Do you know me, dog?" inquired the stranger.

Achmet nodded, moistening lips suddenly dry.

"Are we to die to-night, then?" he asked.

The head under the flowing headdress was shaken.

"Not unless you are fool enough to speak my name. Your companions do not know me. I have not come in my usual capacity, but to guard the prison to-night. Ali Shah fears El Borak might seek to aid you."

"Then El Borak lives!" ejaculated Brent, to whom everything else in the conversation had been unintelligible.

"He still lives." The stranger laughed. "But he will be found, if he is still in the city. If he has fled—well, the passes have been closed by heavy guards, and horsemen are combing the plain and the hills. If he comes here to-night, he will be dealt with. Ali Shah chose to send me rather than a squad of riflemen. Not even the guards know who I am."

As he turned away toward the rear end of the corridor, Brent asked:

"Who is that man?"

But Achmet's flow of conversation had been dried up by the sight of that lean, sardonic face. He shuddered, and drew away from his companions, sitting cross-legged with bowed head. From time to time his shoulders twitched, as if he had seen a reptile or a ghoul.

Brent sighed and stretched himself on the straw. His battered limbs ached, and he was hungry.

Presently he heard the outer door clang. Voices came faintly to him, and the door closed again. Idly he wondered if they were changing the guard. Then he heard the soft rustle of cloth. A man was coming down the corridor. An instant later he came into the range of their vision, and his appearance clutched Brent with an icy dread. Clad in black from head to foot, a spired helmet gave him an appearance of unnatural height. He was enveloped in the folds of a black cloak. But the most sinister implication was in the black mask which fell in loose folds to his breast.

Brent's flesh crawled. Why was that silent, cowled figure coming to their dungeon in the blackness and stillness of the night hours?

The others glared wildly; even Alafdal was shaken out of his daze. Hassan whimpered:

"It is Dhira Azrail!"

But bewilderment mingled with the fear in Achmet's eyes.

The scar-faced stranger came suddenly from the depths of the corridor and confronted the masked man just before the door. The lamplight fell on his face, upon which played a faint, cynical smile.

"What do you wish? I am in charge here."

The masked man's voice was muffled. It sounded cavernous and ghostly, fitting his appearance.

"I am Dhira Azrail. An order has been given. Open the door."

The scarred one salaamed deeply, and murmured: "Hearkening and obedience, my lord!"

He produced a key, turned it in the lock, pulled open the heavy door, and bowed again, humbly indicating for the other to enter. The masked man was moving past him when Achmet came to life startlingly.

"*El Borak!*" he screamed. "Beware! *He* is Dhira Azrail!"

The masked man wheeled like a flash, and the knife the other had aimed at his back glanced from his helmet as he turned. The real Dhira Azrail snarled like a wild cat, but before he could strike again, El Borak's right fist met his jaw with a crushing impact. Flesh, and bone, and consciousness gave way together, and the executioner sagged senseless to the floor.

As Gordon sprang into the cell, the prisoners stumbled dazedly to their feet. Except Achmet, who, knowing that the scarred man was Dhira Azrail, had realized that the

man in the mask must be El Borak—and had acted
accordingly—they did not grasp the situation until
Gordon threw his mask back.

"Can you all walk?" rapped Gordon. "Good! We'll
have to pull out afoot. I couldn't arrange for horses."

Alafdal Khan looked at him dully.

"Why should I go?" he muttered. "Yesterday I had
wealth and power. Now I am a penniless vagabond. If I
leave Rub el Harami, the ameer will cut off my head. It
was an ill day I met you, El Borak! You made a tool of me
for your intrigues."

"So I did, Alafdal Khan." Gordon faced him squarely.
"But I would have made you emir in good truth. The dice
have fallen against us, but our lives remain. And a bold
man can rebuild his fortune. I promise you that if we
escape, the ameer will pardon you and these men."

"His word is not wind," urged Achmet. "He has come
to aid us, when he might have escaped alone. Take heart,
my lord!"

Gordon was stripping the weapons from the senseless
executioner. The man wore two German automatics, a
tulwar, and a curved knife. Gordon gave a pistol to Brent,
and one to Alafdal; Achmet received the tulwar, and
Suleiman the knife, and Gordon gave his own knife to
Hassan. The executioner's garments were given to Brent,
who was practically naked. The oriental garments felt
strange, but he was grateful for their warmth.

The brief struggle had not produced any noise likely to
be overheard by the guard beyond the arched door.
Gordon led his band down the corridor, between rows of
empty cells, until they came to the rear door. There was no
guard outside, as it was deemed too strong to be forced by
anything short of artillery. It was of massive metal,
fastened by a huge bar set in gigantic iron brackets bolted
powerfully into the stone. It took all Gordon's strength to
lift it out of the brackets and lean it against the wall, but
then the door swung silently open, revealing the blackness
of a narrow alley into which they filed.

Gordon pulled the door to behind them. How much leeway they had he did not know. The guard would eventually get suspicious when the supposed Dhira Azrail did not emerge, but he believed it would take them a good while to overcome their almost superstitious dread of the executioner enough to investigate. As for the real Dhira Azrail, he would not recover his senses for hours.

The prison was not far from the west wall. They met no one as they hurried through winding, ill-smelling alleys until they reached the wall at the place where a flight of narrow steps led up to the parapets. Men were patrolling the wall. They crouched in the shadows below the stair and heard the tread of two sentries who met on the firing ledge, exchange muffled greetings, and passed on. As the footsteps dwindled, they glided up the steps. Gordon had secured a rope from an unguarded camel stall. He made it fast by a loose loop to a merlon. One by one they slid swiftly down. Gordon was last, and he flipped the rope loose and coiled it. They might need it again.

They crouched an instant beneath the wall. A wind stole across the plain and stirred Brent's hair. They were free, armed, and outside the devil city. But they were afoot, and the passes were closed against them. Without a word they filed after Gordon across the shadowed plain.

At a safe distance their leader halted, and the men grouped around him, a vague cluster in the starlight.

"All the roads that lead from Rub el Harami are barred against us," he said abruptly. "They've filled the passes with soldiers. We'll have to make our way through the mountains the best way we can. And the only direction in which we can hope to eventually find safety is the east."

"The Great Range bars our path to the east," muttered Alafdal Khan. "Only through the Pass of Nadir Khan may we cross it."

"There is another way," answered Gordon. "It is a pass which lies far to the north of Nadir Khan. There isn't any road leading to it, and it hasn't been used for many generations. But it has a name—the Afridis call it the Pass of Swords—and I've seen it from the east. I've never been west of it before, but maybe I can lead you to it. It lies many days' march from here, through wild mountains which none of us has ever traversed. But it's our only chance. We must have horses and food. Do any of you know where horses can be procured outside the city?"

"Yonder on the north side of the plain," said Achmet, "where a gorge opens from the hills, there dwells a peasant who owns seven horses—wretched, flea-bitten beasts they are, though."

"They must suffice. Lead us to them."

The going was not easy, for the plain was littered with rocks and cut with shallow gullies. All except Gordon were stiff and sore from their beatings, and Hassan's broken arm was a knifing agony to him. It was after more than an hour and a half of tortuous travel that the low mud-and-rock pen loomed before them and they heard the beasts stamping and snorting within it, alarmed by the sounds of their approach. The cluster of buildings squatted in the widening mouth of a shallow canyon, with a shadowy background of bare hills.

Gordon went ahead of the rest, and when the peasant came yawning out of his hut, looking for the wolves he thought were frightening his property, he never saw the tigerish shadow behind him until Gordon's iron fingers shut off his wind. A threat hissed in his ear reduced him to quaking quiescence, though he ventured a wail of protest as he saw other shadowy figures saddling and leading out his beasts.

"Sahibs, I am a poor man! These beasts are not fit for great lords to ride, but they are all of my property! Allah be my witness!"

"Break his head," advised Hassan, whom pain made bloodthirsty.

But Gordon stilled their captive's weeping with a handful of gold which represented at least three times the value of his whole herd. Dazzled by this rich reward, the peasant ceased his complaints, cursed his whimpering wives and children into silence, and at Gordon's order brought forth all the food that was in his hut—leathery loaves of bread, jerked mutton, salt, and eggs. It was little enough with which to start a hard journey. Feed for the horses was slung in a bag behind each saddle, and loaded on the spare horse.

While the beasts were being saddled, Gordon, by the light of a torch held inside a shed by a disheveled woman, whittled splints, tore up a shirt for bandages, and set Hassan's arm—a sickening task, because of the swollen condition of the member. It left Hassan green-faced and gagging, yet he was able to mount with the others.

In the darkness of the small hours they rode up the pathless gorge which led into the trackless hills. Hassan was insistent on cutting the throats of the entire peasant family, but Gordon vetoed this.

"Yes, I know he'll head for the city to betray us, as soon as we get out of sight. But he'll have to go on foot, and we'll lose ourselves in the hills before he gets there."

"There are men trained like bloodhounds in Rub el Harami," said Achmet. "They can track a wolf over bare rock."

Sunrise found them high up in the hills, out of sight of the plain, picking their way up treacherous shale-littered slopes, following dry watercourses, always careful to keep below the sky line as much as possible. Brent was already confused. They seemed lost in a labyrinth of bare hills, in which he was able to recognize general directions only by glimpses of the snow-capped peaks of the Great Range ahead.

As they rode, he studied their leader. There was nothing in Gordon's manner by which he could recognize Shirkuh the Kurd. Gone was the Kurdish accent, the boyish, reckless merry-mad swagger, the peacock vanity of dress, even the wide-legged horseman's stride. The real Gordon was almost the direct antithesis of the rôle he had assumed. In place of the strutting, gaudily clad, braggart youth, there was a direct, hard-eyed man, who wasted no words and about whom there was no trace of egotism or braggadocio. There was nothing of the Oriental about his countenance now, and Brent knew that the mustache alone had not accounted for the perfection of his disguise. That disguise had not depended on any mechanical device; it had been a perfection of mimicry. By no artificial means, but by completely entering into the spirit of the rôle he had assumed, Gordon had altered the expression of his face, his bearing, his whole personality. He had so marvelously portrayed a personality so utterly different from his own, that it seemed impossible that the two were one. Only the eyes were unchanged—the gleaming, untamed black eyes, reflecting a barbarism of vitality and character.

But if not garrulous, Gordon did not prove taciturn, when Brent began to ask questions.

"I was on another trail when I left Kabul," he said. "No need to take up your time with that now. I knew the Black Tigers had a new emir, but didn't know it was Jakrovitch, of course. I'd never bothered to investigate the Black Tigers; didn't consider them important. I left Kabul alone and picked up half a dozen Afridi friends on the way. I became a Kurd after I was well on my road. That's why you lost my trail. None knew me except my Afridis.

"But before I completed my mission, word came through the hills that a Feringi with an escort of Kabuli was looking for me. News travels fast and far through the tribes. I rode back looking for you, and finally sighted you, as a prisoner. I didn't know who'd captured you, but I saw there were too many for us to fight, so I went down to parley. As soon as I saw Muhammad ez Zahir, I guessed who they were, and told them that lie about being lost in the hills and wanting to get to Rub el Harami. I signaled my men—you saw them. They were the men who fired on us as we were coming into the valley where the well was."

"But you shot one of them!"

"I shot over their heads. Just as they purposely missed us. My shots—one, pause, and then three in succession— were a signal that I was going on with the troop, and for

them to return to our rendezvous on Kalat el Jehungir
and wait for me. When one fell forward on his horse, it
was a signal that they understood. We have an elaborate
code of signals, of all kinds.

"I intended trying to get you away that night, but when
you gave me Stockton's message, it changed the situation.
If the new emir was Jakrovitch, I knew what it meant.
Imagine India under the rule of a swine like Jakrovitch!

"I knew that Jakrovitch was after the gold in Shaitan's
Cave. It couldn't be anything else. Oh, yes, I knew the
custom of offering gold each year to the Devil. Stockton
and I had discussed the peril to the peace of Asia if a white
adventurer ever got his hands on it.

"So I knew I'd have to go to Rub el Harami. I didn't
dare tell you who I was—too many men spying around all
the time. When we got to the city, Fate put Alafdal Khan
in my hands. A true Moslem emir is no peril to the Indian
Empire. A real Oriental wouldn't touch Shaitan's gold to
save his life. I meant to make Alafdal emir. I had to tell
him who I was before he'd believe I had a chance of doing
it.

"I didn't premeditatedly precipitate that riot in the *suk*.
I simply took advantage of it. I wanted to get you safely
out of Jakrovitch's hands before I started anything, so I
persuaded Alafdal Kahn that we needed you in our plot,
and he put up the money to buy you. Then during the
auction Jakrovitch lost his head and played into my
hands. Everything would have worked out perfectly, if it
hadn't been for Ali Shah and his man, that Shinwari! It
was inevitable that somebody would recognize me sooner
or later, but I hoped to destroy Jakrovitch, set Alafdal
solidly in power, and have an avenue of escape open for
you and me before that happened."

"At least Jakrovitch is dead," said Brent.

"We didn't fail there," agreed Gordon. "Ali Shah is no
menace to the world. He won't touch the gold. The
organization Jakrovitch built up will fall apart, leaving
only the comparatively harmless core of the Black Tigers

as it was before his coming. We've drawn their fangs, as far as the safety of India is concerned. All that's at stake now are our own lives—but I'll admit I'm selfish enough to want to preserve them."

CHAPTER VIII.

The Pass of Swords

BRENT BEAT HIS numbed hands together for warmth. For days they had been struggling through the trackless hills. The lean horses stumbled against the blast that roared between intervals of breathless sun blaze. The riders clung to the saddles when they could, or stumbled on afoot, leading their mounts, continually gnawed by hunger. At night they huddled together for warmth, men and beasts, in the lee of some rock or cliff, only occasionally finding wood enough to build a tiny fire.

Gordon's endurance was amazing. It was he who led the way, finding water, erasing their too obvious tracks, caring for the mounts when the others were too exhausted to move. He gave his cloak and robe to the ragged Waziris, himself seeming impervious to the chill winds as to the blazing sun.

The pack horse died. There was little food left for the horses, less for the men. They had left the hills now and were in the higher reaches, with the peaks of the Great Range looming through the mists ahead of them. Life became a pain-tinged dream to Brent in which one scene stood out vividly. They sat their gaunt horses at the head of a long valley and saw, far back, white dots moving in the morning mists.

"They have found our trail," muttered Alafdal Khan. "They will not quit it while we live. They have good horses and plenty of food."

And thereafter from time to time they glimpsed, far away and below and behind them, those sinister moving dots, that slowly, slowly cut down the long lead. Gordon ceased his attempts to hide their trail, and they headed straight for the backbone of the range which rose like a rampart before them—scarecrow men on phantom horses, following a grim-faced chief.

On a midday when the sky was as clear as chilled steel, they struggled over a lofty mountain shoulder and sighted a notch that broke the chain of snow-clad summits, and beyond it, the pinnacle of a lesser, more distant peak.

"The Pass of Swords," said Gordon. "The peak beyond it is Kalat el Jehungir, where my men are waiting for me. There will be a man sweeping the surrounding country all the time with powerful field glasses. I don't know whether they can see smoke this far or not, but I'm going to send up a signal for them to meet us at the pass."

Achmet climbed the mountainside with him. The others were too weak for the attempt. High up on the giddy slope they found enough green wood to make a fire that smoked. Presently, manipulated with ragged cloak, balls of thick black smoke rolled upward against the blue. It was the old Indian technique of Gordon's native plains, and Brent knew it was a thousand-to-one shot. Yet hillmen had eyes like hawks.

They descended the shoulder and lost sight of the pass. Then they started climbing once more, over slopes and crags and along the rims of gigantic precipices. It was on one of those ledges that Suleiman's horse stumbled and screamed and went over the edge, to smash to a pulp with its rider a thousand feet below, while the others stared helplessly.

It was at the foot of the long canyon that pitched

upward toward the pass that the starving horses reached the limit of their endurance. The fugitives killed one and haggled off chunks of gristly flesh with their knives. They scorched the meat over a tiny fire, scarcely tasting it as they bolted it. Bodies and nerves were numb for rest and sleep. Brent clung to one thought—if the Afridis had seen the signal, they would be waiting at the pass, with fresh horses. On fresh horses they could escape, for the mounts of their pursuers must be nearly exhausted, too.

On foot they struggled up the steep canyon. Night fell while they struggled, but they did not halt. All through the night they drove their agonized bodies on, and at dawn they emerged from the mouth of the canyon to a broad slope that tilted up to the gap of clear sky cut in the mountain wall. It was empty. The Afridis were not there. Behind them white dots were moving inexorably up the canyon.

"We'll make our last stand at the mouth of the pass," said Gordon.

His eyes swept his phantom crew with a strange remorse. They looked like dead men. They reeled on their feet, their heads swimming with exhaustion and dizziness.

"Sorry about it all," he said. "Sorry, Brent."

"Stockton was my friend," said Brent, and then could have cursed himself, had he had the strength. It sounded so trite, so melodramatic.

"Alafdal, I'm sorry," said Gordon. "Sorry for all you men."

Alafdal lifted his head like a lion throwing back his mane.

"Nay, el Borak! You made a king of me. I was but a glutton and a sot, dreaming dreams I was too timid and too lazy to attempt. You gave me a moment of glory. It is worth all the rest of my life."

Painfully they struggled up to the head of the pass. Brent crawled the last few yards, till Gordon lifted him to his feet. There in the mouth of the great corridor that ran between echoing cliffs, their hair blowing in the icy wind,

they looked back the way they had come and saw their
pursuers, dots no longer, but men on horses. There was a
group of them within a mile, a larger cluster far back
down the canyon. The toughest and best-mounted riders
had drawn away from the others.

The fugitives lay behind boulders in the mouth of the
pass. They had three pistols, a saber, a tulwar, and a knife
between them. The riders had seen their quarry turn at
bay; their rifles glinted in the early-morning light as they
flogged their reeling horses up the slope. Brent recognized
Ali Shah himself, his arm in a sling; Muhammad ez Zahir;
the black-bearded Yusufzai captain. A group of grim
warriors were at their heels. All were gaunt-faced from the
long grind. They came on recklessly, firing as they came.
Yet the men at bay drew first blood.

Alafdal Khan, a poor shot and knowing it, had
exchanged his pistol for Achmet's tulwar. Now Achmet
sighted and fired and knocked a rider out of his saddle
almost at the limit of pistol range. In his exultation he
yelled and incautiously lifted his head above the boulder.
A volley of rifle fire spattered the rock with splashes of hot
lead, and one bullet hit Achmet between the eyes. Alafdal
snatched the pistol as it fell and began firing. His eyes
were bloodshot, his aim wild. But a horse fell, pinning its
rider.

Above the crackling of the Luger came the doomlike
crash of Gordon's Colt. Only the toss of his horse's head
saved Ali Shah. The horse caught the bullet meant for
him, and Ali Shah sprang clear as it fell, rolling to cover.
The others abandoned their horses and followed suit.
They came wriggling up the slope, firing as they came,
keeping to cover.

Brent realized that he was firing the other German
pistol only when he heard a man scream and saw him fall
across a boulder. Vaguely, then, he realized that he had
killed another man. Alafdal Khan had emptied his pistol
without doing much harm. Brent fired and missed, scored
a hit, and missed again. His hand shook with weakness,
and his eyes played him tricks. But Gordon was not

missing. It seemed to Brent that every time the Colt crashed a man screamed and fell. The slope was littered with white-clad figures. They had not worn their black armor on that chase.

Perhaps the madness of the high places had entered Ali Shah's brain on that long pursuit. At any rate he would not wait for the rest of his men, plodding far behind him. Like a madman he drove his warriors to the assault. They came on, firing and dying in the teeth of Gordon's bullets till the slope was a shambles. But the survivors came grimly on, nearer and nearer, and then suddenly they had broken cover and were charging like a gust of hill wind.

Gordon missed Ali Shah with his last bullet and killed the man behind him, and then like ghosts rising from the ground on Judgment Day the fugitives rose and grappled with their pursuers.

Brent fired his last shot full into the face of a savage who rushed at him, clubbing a rifle. Death halted the man's charge, but the rifle stock fell, numbing Brent's shoulder and hurling him to the ground, and there, as he writhed vainly, he saw the brief madness of the fight that raged about him.

He saw the crippled Hassan, snarling like a wounded wolf, beaten down by a Ghilzai who stood with one foot on his neck and repeatedly drove a broken lance through his body. Squirming under the merciless heel, Hassan slashed blindly upward with El Borak's knife in his death agony, and the Ghilzai staggered drunkenly away, blood gushing from the great vein which had been severed behind his knee. He fell dying a few feet from his victim.

Brent saw Ali Shah shoot Alafdal Khan through the body as they came face to face, and Alafdal Khan, dying on his feet, split his enemy's head with one tremendous swing of his tulwar, so they fell together.

Brent saw Gordon cut down the black-bearded Yusufzai captain, and spring at Muhammad ez Zahir with a hate too primitive to accord his foe an honorable death. He parried Muhammad's tulwar and dashed his saber guard into the Afghan's face. Killing his man was not enough for his berserk rage; all his roused passion called for a dog's death for his enemy. And like a raging fury he battered the Afghan back and down with blows of the guard and hilt, refusing to honor him by striking with the blade, until Muhammad fell and lay with broken skull.

Gordon lurched about to face down the slope, the only man on his feet. He stood swaying on wide-braced feet among the dead, and shook the blood from his eyes. They were as red as flame burning on black water. He took a fresh grip on the bloody hilt of his saber, and glared at the horsemen spurring up the canyon—at bay at last, drunken with slaughter, and conscious only of the blind lust to slay and slay before he himself sank in the red welter of his last, grim fight.

Then hoofs rang loud on the rock behind him, and he wheeled, blade lifted—to check suddenly, a wild, blood-stained figure against the sunrise.

"El Borak!"

The pass was filled with shouting. Dimly Brent saw half a dozen horsemen sweep into view. He heard Gordon yell:

"Yar Ali Khan! You saw my signal after all! Give them a volley!"

The banging of their rifles filled the pass with thunder. Brent, twisting his head painfully, saw the demoralization of the Black Tigers. He saw men falling from their saddles, others spurring back down the canyon. Wearied from the long chase, disheartened by the fall of their emir, fearful of a trap, the tired men on tired horses fell back out of range.

Brent was aware of Gordon bending over him, heard him tell the tall Afridi he called Yar Ali Khan to see to the others; heard Yar Ali Khan say they were all dead. Then, as in a dream, Brent felt himself lifted into a saddle, with a man behind to hold him on. Wind blew his hair, and he realized they were galloping. The walls gave back the ring of the flying hoofs, and then they were through the pass, and galloping down the long slope beyond. He saw

Gordon riding near him, on the steed of an Afridi who had mounted before a comrade. And before Brent fainted from sheer exhaustion, he heard Gordon say:

"Let them follow us now if they will; they'll never catch us on their worn-out nags, not in a thousand years!"

And Brent sank into the grateful oblivion of senselessness with his laughter ringing in his ears—the iron, elemental, indomitable laughter of El Borak.

Son of the White Wolf

CHAPTER I.

The Battle Standard

THE COMMANDER OF the Turkish outpost of El Ashraf was awakened before dawn by the stamp of horses and jingle of accoutrements. He sat up and shouted for his orderly. There was no response, so he rose, hurriedly jerked on his garments, and strode out of the mud hut that served as his headquarters. What he saw rendered him momentarily speechless.

His command was mounted, in full marching formation, drawn up near the railroad that it was their duty to guard. The plain to the left of the track where the tents of the troopers had stood now lay bare. The tents had been loaded on the baggage camels which stood fully packed and ready to move out. The commandant glared wildly, doubting his own senses, until his eyes rested on a flag borne by a trooper. The waving pennant did not display the familiar crescent. The commandant turned pale.

"What does this mean?" he shouted, striding forward. His lieutenant, Osman, glanced at him inscrutably. Osman was a tall man, hard and supple as steel, with a dark keen face.

"Mutiny, *effendi*," he replied calmly. "We are sick of this war we fight for the Germans. We are sick of Djemal Pasha and those other fools of the Council of Unity and Progress, and, incidentally, of you. So we are going into the hills to build a tribe of our own."

"Madness!" gasped the officer, tugging at his revolver. Even as he drew it, Osman shot him through the head.

The lieutenant sheathed the smoking pistol and turned to the troopers. The ranks were his to a man, won to his wild ambition under the very nose of the officer who now lay there with his brains oozing.

"Listen!" he commanded.

In the tense silence they all heard the low, deep reverberation in the west.

"British guns!" said Osman. "Battering the Turkish Empire to bits! The New Turks have failed. What Asia needs is not a new party, but a new race! There are thousands of fighting men between the Syrian coast and the Persian highlands, ready to be roused by a new word, a new prophet! The East is moving in her sleep. Ours is the duty to awaken her!

"You have all sworn to follow me into the hills. Let us return to the ways of our pagan ancestors who worshipped the White Wolf on the steppes of High Asia before they bowed to the creed of Mohammed!

"We have reached the end of the Islamic Age. We abjure Allah as a superstition fostered by an epileptic Meccan camel driver. Our people have copied Arab ways too long. But we hundred men are *Turks*! We have burned the Koran. We bow not toward Mecca, nor swear by their false Prophet. And now follow me as we planned—to establish ourselves in a strong position in the hills and to seize Arab women for our wives."

"Our sons will be half Arab," someone protested.

"A man is the son of his father," retorted Osman. "We Turks have always looted the *harims* of the world for our women, but our sons are always Turks.

"Come! We have arms, horses, supplies. If we linger we shall be crushed with the rest of the army between the

British on the coast and the Arabs the Englishman Lawrence is bringing up from the south. On to El Awad! The sword for the men—captivity for the women!"

His voice cracked like a whip as he snapped the orders that set the lines in motion. In perfect order they moved off through the lightening dawn toward the range of saw-edged hills in the distance. Behind them the air still vibrated with the distant rumble of the British artillery. Over them waved a banner that bore the head of a white wolf—the battle-standard of most ancient Turan.

CHAPTER II.

Massacre

WHEN FRAULEIN OLGA VON BRUCKMANN, known as a famous German secret agent, arrived at the tiny Arab hill-village of El Awad, it was in a drizzling rain, that made the dusk a blinding curtain over the muddy town.

With her companion, an Arab named Ahmed, she rode into the muddy street, and the villagers crept from their hovels to stare in awe at the first white woman most of them had ever seen.

A few words from Ahmed and the *shaykh* salaamed and showed her to the best mud hut in the village. The horses were led away to feed and shelter, and Ahmed paused long enough to whisper to his companion:

"El Awad is friendly to the Turks. Have no fear. I shall be near, in any event."

"Try and get fresh horses," she urged. "I must push on as soon as possible."

"The *shaykh* swears there isn't a horse in the village in fit condition to be ridden. He may be lying. But at any rate our own horses will be rested enough to go on by dawn. Even with fresh horses it would be useless to try to go any farther tonight. We'd lose our way among the hills, and in this region there's always the risk of running into Lawrence's Bedouin raiders."

Olga knew that Ahmed knew she carried important secret documents from Baghdad to Damascus, and she knew from experience that she could trust his loyalty. Removing only her dripping cloak and riding boots, she stretched herself on the dingy blankets that served as a bed. She was worn out from the strain of the journey.

She was the first white woman ever to attempt to ride from Baghdad to Damascus. Only the protection accorded a trusted secret agent by the long arm of the German-Turkish government, and her guide's zeal and craft, had brought her thus far in safety.

She fell asleep, thinking of the long weary miles still to be traveled, and even greater dangers, now that she had come into the region where the Arabs were fighting their Turkish masters. The Turks still held the country, that summer of 1917, but lightninglike raids flashed across the desert, blowing up trains, cutting tracks and butchering the inhabitants of isolated posts. Lawrence was leading the tribes northward, and with him was the mysterious American, *El Borak*, whose name was one to hush children.

She never knew how long she slept, but she awoke suddenly and sat up, in fright and bewilderment. The rain still beat on the roof, but there mingled with it shrieks of pain or fear, yells and the staccato crackling of rifles. She sprang up, lighted a candle and was just pulling on her boots when the door was hurled open violently.

Ahmed reeled in, his dark face livid, blood oozing through the fingers that clutched his breast.

"The village is attacked!" he cried chokingly. "Men in Turkish uniform! There must be some mistake! They know El Awad is friendly! I tried to tell their officer we are friends, but he shot me! We must get away, quick!"

A shot cracked in the open door behind him and a jet of fire spurted from the blackness. Ahmed groaned and crumpled. Olga cried out in horror, staring wide-eyed at the figure who stood before her. A tall, wiry man in Turkish uniform blocked the door. He was handsome in a dark, hawklike way, and he eyed her in a manner that brought the blood to her cheeks.

"Why did you kill that man?" she demanded. "He was a trusted servant of your country."

"I have no country," he answered, moving toward her. Outside the firing was dying away and women's voices were lifted piteously. "I go to build one, as my ancestor Osman did."

"I don't know what you're talking about," she retorted. "But unless you provide me with an escort to the nearest post, I shall report you to your superiors, and—"

He laughed wildly at her. "I have no superiors, you little fool! I am an empire builder, I tell you! I have a hundred armed men at my disposal. I'll build a new race in these hills." His eyes blazed as he spoke.

"You're mad!" she exclaimed.

"Mad? It's you who are mad not to recognize the possibilities as I have! This war is bleeding the life out of Europe. When it's over, no matter who wins, the nations will lie prostrate. Then it will be Asia's turn!

"If Lawrence can build up an Arab army to fight for him, then certainly I, an Ottoman, can build up a kingdom among my own peoples! Thousands of Turkish soldiers have deserted to the British. They and more will desert again to me, when they hear that a Turk is building anew the empire of ancient Turan."

"Do what you like," she answered, believing he had been seized by the madness that often grips men in time of war when the world seems crumbling and any wild dream looks possible. "But at least don't interfere with my mission. If you won't give me an escort, I'll go on alone."

"You'll go with me!" he retorted, looking down at her with hot admiration.

Olga was a handsome girl, tall, slender but supple, with a wealth of unruly golden hair. She was so completely feminine that no disguise would make her look like a man, not even the voluminous robes of an Arab, so she had attempted none. She trusted instead to Ahmed's skill to bring her safely through the desert.

"Do you hear those screams? My men are supplying themselves with wives to bear soldiers for the new empire. Yours shall be the signal honor of being the first to go into Sultan Osman's *seraglio*!"

"You do not dare!" She snatched a pistol from her blouse.

Before she could level it he wrenched it from her with brutal strength.

"Dare!" He laughed at her vain struggles. "What do I not dare? I tell you a new empire is being born tonight! Come with me! There's no time for love-making now. Before dawn we must be on the march for Sulaiman's Walls. The star of the White Wolf rises!"

CHAPTER III.

The Call of Blood

THE SUN WAS not long risen over the saw-edged mountains to the east, but already the heat was glazing the cloudless sky to the hue of white-hot steel. Along the dim road that split the immensity of the desert a single shape moved. The shape grew out of the heat-hazes of the south and resolved itself into a man on a camel.

The man was no Arab. His boots and khakis, as well as the rifle-butt jutting from beneath his knee, spoke of the West. But with his dark face and hard frame he did not look out of place, even in that fierce land. He was Francis Xavier Gordon, El Borak, whom men loved, feared or hated, according to their political complexion, from the Golden Horn to the headwaters of the Ganges.

He had ridden most of the night, but his iron frame had not yet approached the fringes of weariness. Another mile, and he sighted a yet dimmer trail straggling down from a range of hills to the east. Something was coming along this trail—a crawling something that left a broad dark smear on the hot flints.

Gordon swung his camel into the trail and a moment

156

later bent over the man who lay there gasping stertorously. It was a young Arab, and the breast of his *abba* was soaked in blood.

"Yusef!" Gordon drew back the wet *abba*, glanced at the bared breast, then covered it again. Blood oozed steadily from a blue-rimmed bullet-hole. There was nothing he could do. Already the Arab's eyes were glazing. Gordon stared up the trail, seeing neither horse nor camel anywhere. But the dark smear stained the stones as far as he could see.

"My God, man, how far have you crawled in this condition?"

"An hour—many hours—I do not know!" panted Yusef. "I fainted and fell from the saddle. When I came to I was lying in the trail and my horse was gone. But I knew you would be coming up from the south, so I crawled—crawled! Allah, how hard are thy stones!"

Gordon set a canteen to his lips and Yusef drank noisily, then clutched Gordon's sleeve with clawing fingers.

"El Borak, I am dying and that is no great matter, but there is the matter of vengeance—not for me, *ya sidi*, but for innocent ones. You know I was on furlough to my village, El Awad. I am the only man of El Awad who fights for Arabia. The elders are friendly to the Turks. But last night the Turks burned El Awad! They marched in before midnight and the people welcomed them—while I hid in a shed.

"Then without warning they began slaying! The men of El Awad were unarmed and helpless. I slew one soldier myself. Then they shot me and I dragged myself away— found my horse and rode to tell the tale before I died. Ah, Allah, I have tasted of perdition this night!"

"Did you recognize their officer?" asked Gordon.

"I never saw him before. They called this leader of theirs Osman Pasha. Their flag bore the head of a white wolf. I saw it by the light of the burning huts. My people cried out in vain that they were friends.

"There was a German woman and a man of Hauran

who came to El Awad from the east, just at nightfall. I
think they were spies. The Turks shot him and took her
captive. It was all blood and madness."

"Mad indeed!" muttered Gordon. Yusef lifted himself
on an elbow and groped for him, a desperate urgency in
his weakening voice.

"El Borak, I fought well for the Emir Feisal, and for
Lawrence *effendi*, and for you! I was at Yenbo, and Wejh,
and Akaba. Never have I asked a reward! I ask now:
justice and vengeance! Grant me this plea: Slay the
Turkish dogs who butchered my people!"

Gordon did not hesitate.

"They shall die," he answered.

Yusef smiled fiercely, gasped: "*Allaho akbat*!" then
sank back dead.

Within the hour Gordon rode eastward. The vultures
had already gathered in the sky with their grisly
foreknowledge of death, then flapped sullenly away from
the cairn of stones he had piled over the dead man, Yusef.

Gordon's business in the north could wait. One reason
for his dominance over the Orientals was the fact that in
some ways his nature closely resembled theirs. He not
only understood the cry for vengeance, but he sympa-
thized with it. And he always kept his promise.

But he was puzzled. The destruction of a friendly
village was not customary, even by the Turks, and
certainly they would not ordinarily have mishandled their
own spies. If they were deserters they were acting in an
unusual manner, for most deserters made their way to
Feisal. And that wolf's head banner?

Gordon knew that certain fanatics in the New Turks
party were trying to erase all signs of Arab culture from
their civilization. This was an impossible task, since that
civilization itself was based on Arabic culture; but he had
heard that in Istambul the radicals even advocated
abandoning Islam and reverting to the paganism of their
ancestors. But he had never believed the tale.

The sun was sinking over the mountains of Edom when
Gordon came to ruined El Awad, in a fold of the bare

hills. For hours before he had marked its location by black dots dropping in the blue. That they did not rise again told him that the village was deserted except for the dead.

As he rode into the dusty street several vultures flapped heavily away. The hot sun had dried the mud, curdled the red pools in the dust. He sat in his saddle a while, staring silently.

He was no stranger to the handiwork of the Turk. He had seen much of it in the long fighting up from Jeddah on the Red Sea. But even so, he felt sick. The bodies lay in the street, headless, disemboweled, hewn asunder—bodies of children, old women and men. A red mist floated before his eyes, so that for a moment the landscape seemed to swim in blood. The slayers were gone; but they had left a plain road for him to follow.

What the signs they had left did not show him, he guessed. The slayers had loaded their female captives on baggage camels, and had gone eastward, deeper into the hills. Why they were following that road he could not guess, but he knew where it led—to the long-abandoned Walls of Sulaiman, by way of the Well of Achmet.

Without hesitation he followed. He had not gone many miles before he passed more of their work—a baby, its brains oozing from its broken head. Some kidnapped woman had hidden her child in her robes until it had been wrenched from her and brained on the rocks, before her eyes.

The country became wilder as he went. He did not halt to eat, but munched dried dates from his pouch as he rode. He did not waste time worrying over the recklessness of his action—one lone American dogging the crimson trail of a Turkish raiding party.

He had no plan; his future actions would depend on the circumstances that arose. But he had taken the death-trail and he would not turn back while he lived. He was no more foolhardy than his grandfather who single-handedly trailed an Apache war-party for days through the Guadalupes and returned to the settlement on the

Pecos with scalps hanging from his belt.

The sun had set and dusk was closing in when Gordon topped a ridge and looked down on the plain whereon stands the Well of Achmet with its straggling palm grove. To the right of that cluster stood the tents, horse lines and camel lines of a well-ordered force. To the left stood a hut used by travelers as a *khan*. The door was shut and a sentry stood before it. While he watched, a man came from the tents with a bowl of food which he handed in at the door.

Gordon could not see the occupant, but he believed it was the German girl of whom Yusef had spoken, though why they should imprison one of their own spies was one of the mysteries of this strange affair. He saw their flag, and could make out a splotch of white that must be the wolf's head. He saw, too, the Arab women, thirty-five or forty of them herded into a pen improvised from bales and pack-saddles. They crouched together dumbly, dazed by their misfortunes.

He had hidden his camel below the ridge, on the western slope, and he lay concealed behind a clump of stunted bushes until night had fallen. Then he slipped down the slope, circling wide to avoid the mounted patrol, which rode leisurely about the camp. He lay prone behind a boulder till it had passed, then rose and stole toward the hut. Fires twinkled in the darkness beneath the palms and he heard the wailing of the captive women.

The sentry before the door of the hut did not see the cat-footed shadow that glided up to the rear wall. As Gordon drew close he heard voices within. They spoke in Turkish.

One window was in the back wall. Strips of wood had been fastened over it, to serve as both pane and bars. Peering between them, Gordon saw a slender girl in a travel-worn riding habit standing before a dark-faced man in a Turkish uniform. There was no insignia to show what his rank had been. The Turk played with a riding whip and his eyes gleamed with cruelty in the light of a candle on a camp table.

"What do I care for the information you bring from Baghdad?" he was demanding. "Neither Turkey nor Germany means anything to me. But it seems, you fail to realize your own position. It is mine to command, you to obey! You are my prisoner, my captive, my slave! It's time you learned what that means. And the best teacher I know is the whip!"

He fairly spat the last word at her and she paled.

"You dare not subject me to this indignity!" she whispered weakly.

Gordon knew this man must be Osman Pasha. He drew his heavy automatic from its scabbard under his armpit and aimed at the Turk's breast through the crack in the window. But even as his finger closed on the trigger he changed his mind. There was the sentry at the door, and a hundred other armed men, within hearing, whom the sound of a shot would bring on the run. He grasped the window bars and braced his legs.

"I see I must dispel your illusions," muttered Osman, moving toward the girl who cowered back until the wall stopped her. Her face was white. She had dealt with many dangerous men in her hazardous career, and she was not easily frightened. But she had never met a man like Osman. His face was a terrifying mask of cruelty; the ferocity that gloats over the agony of a weaker thing shone in his eyes.

Suddenly he had her by the hair, dragging her to him, laughing at her scream of pain. Just then Gordon ripped the strips off the window. The snapping of the wood sounded loud as a gun-shot and Osman wheeled, drawing his pistol, as Gordon came through the window.

The American hit on his feet, leveled automatic checking Osman's move. The Turk froze, his pistol lifted shoulder high, muzzle pointing at the roof. Outside the sentry called anxiously.

"Answer him!" grated Gordon below his breath. "Tell him everything is all right. And drop that gun!"

The pistol fell to the floor and the girl snatched it up.

"Come here, *Fraulein*!"

She ran to him, but in her haste she crossed the line of fire. In that fleeting moment when her body shielded his, Osman acted. He kicked the table and the candle toppled and went out, and simultaneously he dived for the floor. Gordon's pistol roared deafeningly just as the hut was plunged into darkness. The next instant the door crashed inward and the sentry bulked against the starlight, to crumple as Gordon's gun crashed again and yet again.

With a sweep of his arm Gordon found the girl and drew her toward the window. He lifted her through as if she had been a child, and climbed through after her. He did not know whether his blind slug had struck Osman or not. The man was crouching silently in the darkness, but there was no time to strike a match and see whether he was living or dead. But as they ran across the shadowy plain, they heard Osman's voice lifted in passion.

By the time they reached the crest of the ridge the girl was winded. Only Gordon's arm about her waist, half dragging, half carrying, her, enabled her to make the last few yards of the steep incline. The plain below them was alive with torches and shouting men. Osman was yelling for them to run down the fugitives, and his voice came faintly to them on the ridge.

"Take them alive, curse you! Scatter and find them! It's El Borak!" An instant later he was yelling with an edge of panic in his voice: "Wait. Come back! Take cover and make ready to repel an attack! He may have a horde of Arabs with him!"

"He thinks first of his own desires, and only later of the safety of his men," muttered Gordon. "I don't think he'll ever get very far. Come on."

He led the way to the camel, helped the girl into the saddle, then leaped up himself. A word, a tap of the camel wand, and the beast ambled silently off down the slope.

"I know Osman caught you at El Awad," said Gordon. "But what's he up to? What's his game?"

"He was a lieutenant stationed at El Ashraf," she answered. "He persuaded his company to mutiny, kill their commander and desert. He plans to fortify the Walls of Sulaiman, and build a new empire. I thought at first he was mad, but he isn't. He's a devil."

"The Walls of Sulaiman?" Gordon checked his mount and sat for a moment motionless in the starlight.

"Are you game for an all-night ride?" he asked presently.

"Anywhere! As long as it is far away from Osman!" There was a hint of hysteria in her voice.

"I doubt if your escape will change his plans. He'll probably lie about Achmet all night under arms expecting an attack. In the morning he will decide that I was alone, and pull out for the Walls.

"Well, I happen to know that an Arab force is there, waiting for an order from Lawrence to move on to Ageyli. Three hundred Juheina camel-riders, sworn to Feisal. Enough to eat Osman's gang. Lawrence's messenger should reach them some time between dawn and noon. There is a chance we can get there before the Juheina pull out. If we can, we'll turn them on Osman and wipe him out, with his whole pack.

"It won't upset Lawrence's plans for the Juheina to get to Ageyli a day late, and Osman must be destroyed. He's a mad dog running loose."

"His ambition sounds mad," she murmured. "But when he speaks of it, with his eyes blazing, it's easy to believe he might even succeed."

"You forget that crazier things have happened in the desert," he answered, as he swung the camel eastward. "The world is being made over here, as well as in Europe. There's no telling what damage this Osman might do, if left to himself. The Turkish Empire is falling to pieces, and new empires have risen out of the ruins of old ones.

"But if we can get to Sulaiman before the Juheina march, we'll check him. If we find them gone, we'll be in a pickle ourselves. It's a gamble, our lives against his. Are you game?"

"Till the last card falls!" she retorted. His face was a blur in the starlight, but she sensed rather than saw his grim smile of approval.

The camel's hoofs made no sound as they dropped down the slope and circled far wide of the Turkish camp. Like ghosts on a ghost-camel they moved across the plain under the stars. A faint breeze stirred the girl's hair. Not until the fires were dim behind them and they were again climbing a hill-road did she speak.

"I know you. You're the American they call El Borak, the Swift. You came down from Afghanistan when the war began. You were with King Hussein even before Lawrence came over from Egypt. Do you know who I am?"

"Yes."

"Then what's my status?" she asked. "Have you rescued me or captured me? Am I a prisoner?"

"Let us say companion, for the time being," he suggested. "We're up against a common enemy. No reason why we shouldn't make common cause, is there?"

"None!" she agreed, and leaning her blond head against his hard shoulder, she went soundly to sleep.

A gaunt moon rose, pushing back the horizons, flooding craggy slopes and dusty plains with leprous silver. The vastness of the desert seemed to mock the tiny figures on their tiring camel, as they rode blindly on toward what Fate they could not guess.

CHAPTER IV.

Wolves of the Desert

OLGA AWOKE AS dawn was breaking. She was cold and stiff, in spite of the cloak Gordon had wrapped about her, and she was hungry. They were riding through a dry gorge with rock-strewn slopes rising on either hand, and the camel's gait had become a lurching walk. Gordon halted it, slid off without making it kneel, and took its rope.

"It's about done, but the Walls aren't far ahead. Plenty of water there—food, too, if the Juheina are still there. There are dates in that pouch."

If he felt the strain of fatigue he did not show it as he strode along at the camel's head. Olga rubbed her chill hands and wished for sunrise.

"The Well of Harith," Gordon indicated a walled enclosure ahead of them. "The Turks built that wall, years ago, when the Walls of Sulaiman were an army post. Later they abandoned both positions."

The wall, built of rocks and dried mud, was in good shape, and inside the enclosure there was a partly ruined hut. The well was shallow, with a mere trickle of water at the bottom.

165

"I'd better get off and walk too," Olga suggested.

"These flints would cut your boots and feet to pieces. It's not far now. Then the camel can rest all it needs."

"And if the Juheina aren't there—" She left the sentence unfinished.

He shrugged his shoulders.

"Maybe Osman won't come up before the camel's rested."

"I believe he'll make a forced march," she said, not fearfully, but calmly stating an opinion. "His beasts are good. If he drives them hard, he can get here before midnight. Our camel won't be rested enough to carry us, by that time. And we couldn't get away on foot, in this desert."

He laughed, and respecting her courage, did not try to make light of their position.

"Well," he said quietly, "let's hope the Juheina are still there!"

If they were not, she and Gordon were caught in a trap of hostile, waterless desert, fanged with the long guns of predatory tribesmen.

Three miles further east the valley narrowed and the floor pitched upward, dotted by dry shrubs and boulders. Gordon pointed suddenly to a faint ribbon of smoke feathering up into the sky.

"Look! The Juheina are there!"

Olga gave a deep sigh of relief. Only then did she realize how desperately she had been hoping for some such sign. She felt like shaking a triumphant fist at the rocky waste about her, as if at a sentient enemy, sullen and cheated of its prey.

Another mile and they topped a ridge and saw a large enclosure surrounding a cluster of wells. There were Arabs squatting about their tiny cooking fires. As the travelers came suddenly into view within a few hundred yards of them, the Bedouins sprang up, shouting. Gordon drew his breath suddenly between clenched teeth.

"They're not Juheina! They're Rualla! Allies of the Turks!"

Too late to retreat. A hundred and fifty wild men were on their feet, glaring, rifles cocked.

Gordon did the next best thing and went leisurely toward them. To look at him one would have thought that he had expected to meet these men here, and anticipated nothing but a friendly greeting. Olga tried to imitate his tranquility, but she knew their lives hung on the crook of a trigger finger. These men were supposed to be her allies, but her recent experience made her distrust Orientals. The sight of these hundreds of wolfish faces filled her with sick dread.

They were hesitating, rifles lifted, nervous and uncertain as surprised wolves, then:

"*Allah*! howled a tall, scarred warrior. "It is El Borak!"

Olga caught her breath as she saw the man's finger quiver on his rifle-trigger. Only a racial urge to gloat over his victim kept him from shooting the American then and there.

"El Borak!" The shout was a wave that swept the throng.

Ignoring the clamor, the menacing rifles, Gordon made the camel kneel and lifted Olga off. She tried, with fair success, to conceal her fear of the wild figures that crowded about them, but her flesh crawled at the blood-lust burning redly in each wolfish eye.

Gordon's rifle was in its boot on the saddle, and his pistol was out of sight, under his shirt. He was careful not to reach for the rifle—a move which would have brought a hail of bullets—but having helped the girl down, he turned and faced the crowd casually, his hands empty. Running his glance over the fierce faces, he singled out a tall stately man in the rich garb of a *shaykh*, who was standing somewhat apart.

"You keep poor watch, Mitkhal ibn Ali," said Gordon. "If I had been a raider your men would be lying in their blood by this time."

Before the *shaykh* could answer, the man who had first recognized Gordon thrust himself violently forward, his face convulsed with hate.

"You expected to find friends here, El Borak!" he
exulted. "But you come too late! Three hundred Juheina
dogs rode north an hour before dawn! We saw them go,
and came up after they had gone. Had they known of your
coming, perhaps they would have stayed to welcome
you!"

"It's not to you I speak, Zangi Khan, you Kurdish
dog," retorted Gordon contemptuously, "but to the
Rualla—honorable men and fair foes!"

Zangi Khan snarled like a wolf and threw up his rifle,
but a lean Bedouin caught his arm.

"Wait!" he growled. "Let El Borak speak. His words
are not wind."

A rumble of approval came from the Arabs. Gordon
had touched their fierce pride and vanity. That would not
save his life, but they were willing to listen to him before
they killed him.

"If you listen he will trick you with cunning words!"
shouted the angered Zangi Khan furiously. "Slay him
now, before he can do us harm!"

"Is Zangi Khan *shaykh* of the Rualla that he gives
commands while Mitkhal stands silent?" asked Gordon
with biting irony.

Mitkhal reacted to his taunt exactly as Gordon knew
he would.

"Let El Borak speak!" he ordered. "I command here,
Zangi Khan! Do not forget that."

"I do not forget, *ya sidi*," the Kurd assured him, but his
eyes burned red at the rebuke. "I but spoke in zeal for your
safety."

Mitkhal gave him a slow, searching glance which told
Gordon that there was no love lost between the two men.
Zangi Khan's reputation as a fighting man meant much to
the younger warriors. Mitkhal was more fox than wolf,
and he evidently feared the Kurd's influence over his men.
As an agent of the Turkish government Zangi's authority
was theoretically equal to Mitkhal's.

Actually this amounted to little, but Mitkhal's

tribesmen took orders from their *shaykh* only. But it put
Zangi in a position to use his personal talents to gain an
ascendency—an ascendency Mitkhal feared would
relegate him to a minor position.

"Speak, El Borak," ordered Mitkhal. "But speak
swiftly. It may be," he added, "Allah's will that the
moments of your life are few."

"Death marches from the west," said Gordon abruptly.
"Last night a hundred Turkish deserters butchered the
people of El Awad."

"*Wallah!*" swore a tribesman. "El Awad was friendly
to the Turks!"

"A lie!" cried Zangi Khan. "Or if true, the dogs of
deserters slew the people to curry favor with Feisal."

"When did men come to Feisal with the blood of
children on their hands?" retorted Gordon. "They have
foresworn Islam and worship the White Wolf. They
carried off the young women and the old women, the men
and the children they slew like dogs."

A murmur of anger rose from the Arabs. The Bedouins
had a rigid code of warfare, and they did not kill women
or children. It was the unwritten law of the desert, old
when Abraham came up out of Chaldea.

But Zangi Khan cried out in angry derision, blind to
the resentful looks cast at him. He did not understand that
particular phase of the Bedouins' code, for his people had
no such inhibition. Kurds in war killed women as well as
men.

"What are the women of El Awad to us?" he sneered.

"Your heart I know already," answered Gordon with
icy contempt. "It is to the Rualla that I speak."

"A trick!" howled the Kurd. "A lie to trick us!"

"It is no lie!" Olga stepped forward boldly. "Zangi
Khan, you know that I am an agent of the German
government. Osman Pasha, leader of these renegades
burned El Awad last night, as El Borak has said. Osman
murdered Ahmed ibn Shalaan, my guide, among others.
He is as much our enemy as he is an enemy of the British."

She looked to Mitkhal for help, but the *shaykh* stood apart, like an actor watching a play in which he had not yet received his cue.

"What if it is the truth?" Zangi Khan snarled, muddled by his hate and fear of El Borak's cunning. "What is El Awad to us?"

Gordon caught him up instantly.

"This Kurd asks what is the destruction of a friendly village! Doubtless, naught to him! But what does it mean to you, who have left your herds and families unguarded? If you let this pack of mad dogs range the land, how can you be sure of the safety of your wives and children?"

"What would you have, El Borak?" demanded a grey-bearded raider.

"Trap these Turks and destroy them. I'll show you how."

It was then that Zangi Khan lost his head completely.

"Heed him not!" he screamed. "Within the hour we must ride northward! The Turks will give us ten thousand British pounds for his head!"

Avarice burned briefly in the men's eyes, to be dimmed by the reflection that the reward, offered for El Borak's head, would be claimed by the *shaykh* and Zangi. They made no move and Mitkhal stood aside with an air of watching a contest that did not concern himself.

"Take his head!" screamed Zangi, sensing hostility at last, and thrown into a panic by it.

His demoralization was completed by Gordon's taunting laugh.

"You seem to be the only one who wants my head, Zangi! Perhaps you can take it!"

Zangi howled incoherently, his eyes glaring red, then threw up his rifle, hip-high. Just as the muzzle came up, Gordon's automatic crashed thunderously. He had drawn so swiftly not a man there had followed his motion. Zangi Khan reeled back under the impact of hot lead, toppled sideways and lay still.

In an instant a hundred cocked rifles covered Gordon.

Confused by varying emotions, the men hesitated for the fleeting instant it took Mitkhal to shout:

"Hold! Do not shoot!"

He strode forward with the air of a man ready to take the center of the stage at last, but he could not disguise the gleam of satisfaction in his shrewd eyes.

"No man here is kin to Zangi Khan," he said offhandedly. "There is no cause for blood feud. He had eaten the salt, but he attacked our prisoner whom he thought unarmed."

He held out his hand for the pistol, but Gordon did not surrender it.

"I'm not your prisoner," said he. "I could kill you before your men could lift a finger. But I didn't come here to fight you. I came asking aid to avenge the children and women of my enemies. I risk my life for your families. Are you dogs, to do less?"

The question hung in the air unanswered, but he had struck the right chord in their barbaric bosoms, that were always ready to respond to some wild deed of reckless chivalry. Their eyes glowed and they looked at their *shaykh* expectantly.

Mitkhal was a shrewd politician. The butchery at El Awad meant much less to him than it meant to his younger warriors. He had associated with so-called civilized men long enough to lose much of his primitive integrity. But he always followed the side of public opinion, and was shrewd enough to lead a movement he could not check. Yet, he was not to be stampeded into a hazardous adventure.

"These Turks may be too strong for us," he objected.

"I'll show you how to destroy them with little risk," answered Gordon. "But there must be covenants between us, Mitkhal."

"These Turks must be destroyed," said Mitkhal, and he spoke sincerely there, at least. "But there are too many blood feuds between us, El Borak, for us to let you get out of our hands."

Gordon laughed.

"You can't whip the Turks without my help and you know it. Ask your young men what they desire!"

"Let El Borak lead us!" shouted a young warrior instantly. A murmur of approval paid tribute to Gordon's widespread reputation as a strategist.

"Very well!" Mitkhal took the tide. "Let there be truce between us—with conditions! Lead us against the Turks. If you win, you and the woman shall go free. If we lose, we take your head!"

Gordon nodded, and the warriors yelled in glee. It was just the sort of a bargain that appealed to their minds, and Gordon knew it was the best he could make.

"Bring bread and salt!" ordered Mitkhal, and a giant black slave moved to do his bidding. "Until the battle is lost or won there is truce between us, and no Rualla shall harm you, unless you spill Rualla blood."

Then he thought of something else and his brow darkened as he thundered:

"Where is the man who watched from the ridge?"

A terrified youth was pushed forward. He was a member of a small tribe tributary to the more important Rualla.

"Oh, *shaykh*," he faltered, "I was hungry and stole away to a fire for meat—"

"Dog!" Mitkhal struck him in the face. "Death is thy portion for failing in thy duty."

"Wait!" Gordon interposed. "Would you question the will of Allah? If the boy had not deserted his post he would have seen us coming up the valley, and your men would have fired on us and killed us. Then you would not have been warned of the Turks, and would have fallen prey to them before discovering they were enemies. Let him go and give thanks to Allah Who sees all!"

It was the sort of sophistry that appeals to the Arab mind. Even Mitkhal was impressed.

"Who knows the mind of Allah?" he conceded. "Live, Musa, but next time perform the will of Allah with vigilance and a mind to orders. And now, El Borak, let us discuss battle-plans while food is prepared."

CHAPTER V.

Treachery

IT WAS NOT yet noon when Gordon halted the Rualla beside the Well of Harith. Scouts sent westward reported no sign of the Turks, and the Arabs went forward with the plans made before leaving the Walls—plans outlined by Gordon and agreed to by Mitkhal. First the tribesmen began gathering rocks and hurling them into the well.

"The water's still beneath," Gordon remarked to Olga. "But it'll take hours of hard work to clean out the well so that anybody can get to it. The Turks can't do it under our rifles. If we win, we'll clean it out ourselves, so the next travelers won't suffer."

"Why not take refuge in the *sangar* ourselves?" she asked.

"Too much of a trap. That's what we're using it for. We'd have no chance with them in open fight, and if we laid an ambush out in the valley, they'd simply fight their way through us. But when a man's shot at in the open, his first instinct is to make for the nearest cover. So I'm hoping to trick them into going into the *sangar*. Then we'll bottle them up and pick them off at our leisure. Without

173

water they can't hold out long. We shouldn't lose a dozen men, if any."

"It seems strange to see you solicitous about the lives of these Rualla, who are your enemies, after all," she laughed.

"Instinct, maybe. No man fit to lead wants to lose any more of them then he can help. Just now these men are my allies, and it's up to me to protect them as well as I can. I'll admit I'd rather be fighting with the Juheina. Feisal's messenger must have started for the Walls hours before I supposed he would."

"And if the Turks surrender, what then?"

"I'll try to get them to Lawrence—all but Osman Pasha." Gordon's face darkened. "That man hangs if he falls into my hands."

"How will you get them to Lawrence? The Rualla won't take them."

"I haven't the slightest idea. But let's catch our hare before we start broiling him. Osman may whip the daylights out of us."

"It means your head if he does," she warned with a shudder.

"Well, it's worth ten thousand pounds to the Turks," he laughed, and moved to inspect the partly ruined hut. Olga followed him.

Mitkhal, directing the blocking of the well, glanced sharply at them, then noted that a number of men were between them and the gate, and turned back to his overseeing.

"*Hsss*, El Borak!" It was a tense whisper, just as Gordon and Olga turned to leave the hut. An instant later they located a tousled head thrust up from behind a heap of rubble. It was the boy Musa who obviously had slipped into the hut through a crevice in the back wall.

"Watch from the door and warn me if you see anybody coming," Gordon muttered to Olga. "This lad may have something to tell."

"I have, *effendi*!" The boy was trembling with excitement. "I overheard the *shaykh* talking secretly to his black slave, Hassan. I saw them walk away among the palms while you and the woman were eating, at the Walls, and I crept after them, for I feared they meant you mischief—and you saved my life.

"El Borak, listen! Mitkah means to slay you, whether you win this battle for him or not! He was glad you slew the Kurd, and he is glad to have your aid in wiping out these Turks. But he lusts for the gold the other Turks will pay for your head. Yet he dares not break his word and the covenant of the salt openly. So, if we win the battle, Hassan is to shoot you, and swear you fell by a Turkish bullet!"

The boy rushed on with his story:

"Then Mitkhal will say to the people: 'El Borak was our guest and ate our salt. But now he is dead, through no fault of ours, and there is no use wasting the reward. So we will take off his head and take it to Damascus and the Turks will give us ten thousand pounds.'"

Gordon smiled grimly at Olga's horror. That was typical Arab logic.

"It didn't occur to Mitkhal that Hassan might miss his first shot and not get a chance to shoot again, I suppose?" he suggested.

"Oh, yes, *effendi*, Mitkhal thinks of everything. If you kill Hassan, Mitkhal will swear you broke the covenant yourself, by spilling the blood of a Rualla, or a Rualla's servant, which is the same thing, and will feel free to order you beheaded."

There was genuine humor in Gordon's laugh.

"Thanks, Musa! If I saved your life, you've paid me back. Better get out now, before somebody sees you talking to us."

"What shall we do?" exclaimed Olga, pale to the lips.

"You're in no danger," he assured her.

She colored angrily.

"I wasn't thinking of that! Do you think I have less gratitude than that Arab boy? That *shaykh* means to murder you, don't you understand? Let's steal camels and run for it!"

"Run where? If we did, they'd be on our heels in no time, deciding I'd lied to them about everything. Anyway, we wouldn't have a chance. They're watching us too closely. Besides, I wouldn't run if I could. I started to wipe out Osman Pasha, and this is the best chance I see to do it. Come on. Let's get out in the *sangar* before Mitkhal gets suspicious."

As soon as the well was blocked the men retired to the hillsides. Their camels were hidden behind the ridges, and the men crouched behind rocks and among the stunted shrubs along the slopes. Olga refused Gordon's offer to send her with an escort back to the Walls, and stayed with him taking up a position behind a rock, Osman's pistol in her belt. They lay flat on the ground and the heat of the sun-baked flints seeped through their garments.

Once she turned her head, and shuddered to see the blank black countenance of Hassan regarding them from some bushes a few yards behind them. The black slave, who knew no law but his master's command, was determined not to let Gordon out of his sight.

She spoke of this in a low whisper to the American.

"Sure," he murmured. "I saw him. But he won't shoot till he knows which way the fight's going, and is sure none of the men are looking."

Olga's flesh crawled in anticipation of more horrors. If they lost the fight the enraged Ruallas would tear Gordon to pieces, supposing he survived the encounter. If they won, his reward would be a treacherous bullet in the back.

The hours dragged slowly by. Not a flutter of cloth, no lifting of an impudent head betrayed the presence of the wild men on the slopes. Olga began to feel her nerves quiver. Doubts and forebodings gnawed maddeningly at her.

"We took position too soon! The men will lose patience. Osman can't get here before midnight. It took us all night to reach the Well."

"Bedouins never lose patience when they smell loot," he answered. "I believe Osman will get here before sundown. We made poor time on a tiring camel for the last few hours of that ride. I believe Osman broke camp before dawn and pushed hard."

Another thought came to torture her.

"Suppose he doesn't come at all? Suppose he has changed his plans and gone somewhere else? The Rualla will believe you lied to them!"

"Look!"

The sun hung low in the west, a fiery, dazzling ball. She blinked, shading her eyes.

Then the head of a marching column grew out of the dancing heat-waves: lines of horsemen, grey with dust, files of heavily laden baggage camels, with the captive women riding them. The standard hung loose in the breathless air; but once, when a vagrant gust of wind, hot as the breath of perdition, lifted the folds, the white wolf's head was displayed.

Crushing proof of idolatry and heresy! In their agitation the Rualla almost betrayed themselves. Even Mitkhal turned pale.

"Allah! Sacrilege! Forgotten of God. Hell shall be thy portion!"

"Easy!" hissed Gordon, feeling the semi-hysteria that ran down the lurking lines. "Wait for my signal. They may halt to water their camels at the Well."

Osman must have driven his people like a fiend all day. The women drooped on the loaded camels; the dust-caked faces of the soldiers were drawn. The horses reeled with weariness. But it was soon evident that they did not intend halting at the Well with their goal, the Walls of Sulaiman, so near. The head of the column was even with the *sangar* when Gordon fired. He was aiming at Osman, but the range was long, the sun-glare on the rocks dazzling. The man behind Osman fell, and at the signal the slopes came alive with spurting flame.

The column staggered. Horses and men went down and stunned soldiers gave back a ragged fire that did no harm. They did not even see their assailants save as bits of white cloth bobbing among the boulders.

Perhaps discipline had grown lax during the grind of

that merciless march. Perhaps panic seized the tired Turks. At any rate the column broke and men fled toward the *sangar* without waiting for orders. They would have abandoned the baggage camels had no Osman ridden among them. Cursing and striking with the flat of his saber, he made them drive the beasts in with them.

"I hoped they'd leave the camels and women outside," grunted Gordon. "Maybe they'll drive them out when they find there's no water."

The Turks took their positions in good order, dismounting and ranging along the wall. Some dragged the Arab women off the camels and drove them into the hut. Others improvised a pen for the animals with stakes and ropes between the back of the hut and the wall. Saddles were piled in the gate to complete the barricade.

The Arabs yelled taunts as they poured in a hail of lead, and a few leaped up and danced derisively, waving their rifles. But they stopped that when a Turk drilled one of them cleanly through the head. When the demonstrations ceased, the besiegers offered scanty targets to shoot at.

However, the Turks fired back frugally and with no indication of panic, now that they were under cover and fighting the sort of a fight they understood. They were well protected by the wall from the men directly in front of them, but those facing north could be seen by the men on the south ridge, and vice versa. But the distance was too great for consistently effective shooting at these marks by the Arabs.

"We don't seem to be doing much damage," remarked Olga presently.

"Thirst will win for us," Gordon answered. "All we've got to do is to keep them bottled up. They probably have enough water in their canteens to last through the rest of the day. Certainly no longer. Look, they're going to the well now."

The well stood in the middle of the enclosure, in a comparatively exposed area, as seen from above. Olga saw men approaching it with canteens in their hands, and the Arabs, with sardonic enjoyment, refrained from firing

at them. They reached the well, and then the girl saw the
change come over them. It ran through their band like an
electric shock. The men along the walls reacted by firing
wildly. A furious yelling rose, edged with hysteria, and
men began to run madly about the enclosure. Some
toppled, hit by shots dropping from the ridges.

"What are they doing?" Olga started to her knees, and
was instantly jerked down again by Gordon. The Turks
were running into the hut. If she had been watching
Gordon she would have sensed the meaning of it, for his
dark face grew suddenly grim.

"They're dragging the women out!" she exclaimed. "I
see Osman waving his saber. What? Oh, God! They're
butchering the women!"

Above the crackle of shots rose terrible shrieks and the
sickening *chack* of savagely driven blows. Olga turned
sick and hid her face. Osman had realized the trap into
which he had been driven, and his reaction was that of a
mad dog. Recognizing defeat in the blocked well, facing
the ruin of his crazy ambitions by thirst and Bedouin
bullets, he was taking this vengeance on the whole Arab
race.

On all sides the Arabs rose howling, driven to frenzy by
the sight of that slaughter. That these women were of
another tribe made no difference. A stern chivalry was the
foundation of their society, just as it was among the
frontiersmen of early America. There was no sentimental-
ism about it. It was real and vital as life itself.

The Rualla went beserk when they saw women of their
race falling under the swords of the Turks. A wild yell
shattered the brazen sky, and recklessly breaking cover,
the Arabs pelted down the slopes, howling like fiends.
Gordon could not check them, nor could Mitkhal. Their
shouts fell on deaf ears. The walls vomited smoke and
flame as withering volleys raked the oncoming hordes.
Dozens fell, but enough were left to reach the wall and
sweep over it in a wave that neither lead nor steel could
halt.

And Gordon was among them. When he saw he could

not stop the storm he joined it. Mitkhal was not far behind him, cursing his men as he ran. The *shaykh* had no stomach for this kind of fighting, but his leadership was at stake. No man who hung back in this charge would ever be able to command the Rualla again.

Gordon was among the first to reach the wall, leaping over the writhing bodies of half a dozen Arabs. He had not blazed away wildly as he ran like the Bedouins, to reach the wall with an empty gun. He held his fire until the flame spurts from the barrier were almost burning his face, and then emptied his rifle in a point-blank fusilade that left a bloody gap where there had been a line of fierce dark faces an instant before. Before the gap could be closed he had swarmed over and in, and the Rualla poured after him.

As his feet hit the ground a rush of men knocked him against the wall and a blade, thrusting for his life, broke against the rocks. He drove his shortened butt into a snarling face, splintering teeth and bones, and the next instant a surge of his own men over the wall cleared a space about him. He threw away his broken rifle and drew his pistol.

The Turks had been forced back from the wall in a dozen places now, and men were fighting all over the *sangar*. No quarter was asked—none given. The pitiful headless bodies sprawled before the blood-stained hut had turned the Bedouins into hot-eyed demons. The guns were empty now, all but Gordon's automatic. The yells had died down to grunts, punctuated by death-howls. Above these sounds rose the chopping impact of flailing blades, the crunch of fiercely driven rifle butts. So grimly had the Bedouins suffered in that brainless rush, that now they were outnumbered, and the Turks fought with the fury of desperation.

It was Gordon's automatic, perhaps, that tipped the balance. He emptied it without haste and without hesitation, and at that range he could not miss. He was aware of a dark shadow forever behind him, and turned once to see black Hassan following him, smiting methodically right and left with a heavy scimitar already dripping crimson. Even in the fury of the strife, Gordon grinned. The literal-minded Soudanese was obeying instructions to keep at El Borak's heels. As long as the battle hung in doubt, he was Gordon's protector—ready to become his executioner the instant the tide turned in their favor.

"Faithful servant," called Gordon sardonically. "Have a care lest these Turks cheat you of my head!"

Hassan grinned, speechless. Suddenly blood burst from his thick lips and he buckled at the knees. Somewhere in that rush down the hill his black body had stopped a bullet. As he struggled on all fours a Turk ran in from the side and brained him with a rifle-butt. Gordon killed the Turk with his last bullet. He felt no grudge against Hassan. The man had been a good soldier, and had obeyed orders given him.

The *sangar* was a shambles. The men on their feet were less than those on the ground, and all were streaming blood. The white wolf standard had been torn from its staff and lay trampled under vengeful feet. Gordon bent, picked up a saber and looked about for Osman. He saw Mitkhal, running toward the horse-pen, and then he yelled a warning, for he saw Osman.

The man broke away from a group of struggling figures and ran for the pen. He tore away the ropes and the horses, frantic from the noise and smell of blood, stampeded into the *sangar*, knocking men down and trampling them. As they thundered past, Osman, with a magnificent display of agility, caught a handful of flying mane and leaped on the back of the racing steed.

Mitkhal ran toward him, yelling furiously, and snapping a pistol at him. The *shaykh*, in the confusion of the fighting, did not seem to be aware that the gun was empty, for he pulled the trigger again and again as he stood in the path of the oncoming rider. Only at the last moment did he realize his peril and leap back. Even so, he would have sprung clear had not his sandal heel caught in a dead man's *abba*.

Mitkhal stumbled, avoided the lashing hoofs, but not the down-flailing saber in Osman's hand. A wild cry went up from the Rualla as Mitkhal fell, his turban suddenly crimson. The next instant Osman was out of the gate and riding like the wind—straight up the hillside to where he saw the slim figure of the girl to whom he now attributed his overthrow.

Olga had come out from behind the rocks and was standing in stunned horror watching the fight below. Now she awoke suddenly to her own peril at the sight of the madman charging up the slope. She drew the pistol Gordon had taken from him and opened fire. She was not a very good shot. Three bullets missed, the fourth killed the horse, and then the gun jammed. Gordon was running up the slope as the Apaches of his native Southwest run, and behind him streamed a swarm of Rualla. There was not a loaded gun in the whole horde.

Osman took a shocking fall when his horse turned a somersault under him, but rose, bruised and bloody, with Gordon still some distance away. But the Turk had to play hide-and-seek for a few moments among the rocks with his prey before he was able to grasp her hair and twist her screaming to her knees and then he paused an instant to enjoy her despair and terror. That pause was his undoing.

As he lifted his saber to strike off her head, steel clanged loud on steel. A numbing shock ran through his arm and his blade was knocked from his hand. His weapon rang on the hot flints. He whirled to face the blazing slits that were El Borak's eyes. The muscles stood out in cords and ridges on Gordon's sunburnt forearm in the intensity of his passion.

"Pick it up, you filthy dog," he said between his teeth.

Osman hesitated, stooped, caught up the saber and slashed at Gordon's legs without straightening. Gordon leaped back, then sprang in again the instant his toes touched the earth. His return was as paralyzingly quick as the death-leap of a wolf. It caught Osman off balance, his sword extended. Gordon's blade hissed as it cut the air, slicing through flesh, gritting through bone.

The Turk's head toppled from the severed neck and fell at Gordon's feet, the headless body collapsing in a heap. With an excess spasm of hate, Gordon kicked the head savagely down the slope.

"Oh!" Olga turned away and hid her face. But the girl knew that Osman deserved any fate that could have overtaken him. Presently she was aware of Gordon's hand resting lightly on her shoulder and she looked up, ashamed of her weakness. The sun was just dipping below the western ridges. Musa came limping up the slope, blood-stained but radiant.

"The dogs are all dead, *effendi!*" he cried, industriously shaking a plundered watch, in an effort to make it run. "Such of our warriors as still live are faint from strife, and many sorely wounded. There is none to command now but thou."

"Sometimes problems settle themselves," mused Gordon. "But at a ghastly price. If the Rualla hadn't made that rush, which was the death of Hassan and Mitkhal— oh, well, such things are in the hands of Allah, as the Arabs say. A hundred better men than I have died today, but by the decree of some blind Fate, I live."

Gordon looked down on the wounded men. He turned to Musa.

"We must load the wounded on camels," he said, "and take them to the camp at the Walls where there's water and shade. Come."

As they started down the slope he said to Olga, "I'll have to stay with them till they're settled at the Walls, then I must start for the coast. Some of the Rualla will be able to ride, though, and you need have no fear of them. They'll escort you to the nearest Turkish outpost."

She looked at him in surprise.

"Then I'm not your prisoner?"

He laughed.

"I think you can help Feisal more by carrying out your original instructions of supplying misleading information to the Turks! I don't blame you for not confiding even in me. You have my deepest admiration, for you're playing the most dangerous game a woman can."

"Oh!" She felt a sudden warm flood of relief and gladness that he should know she was not really an enemy. Musa was well out of ear-shot. "I might have known you were high enough in Feisal's councils to know that I really am—"

"Gloria Willoughby, the cleverest, most daring secret agent the British government employs," he murmured. The girl impulsively placed her slender fingers in his, and hand in hand they went down the slope together.